9-03

Teenage Mermaid

Ellen Schreiber

Teenage Mermaid

HarperCollins*Publishers*

Library of Congress Cataloging-in-Publication Data
Schreiber, Ellen.
Teenage mermaid / Ellen Schreiber.— 1st ed.
     p.   cm.
Summary: Fifteen-year-old Spencer falls in love with Lilly, a mer-
maid who rescues him from drowning and who returns to land to
find him.
ISBN 0-06-008204-6—ISBN 0-06-008205-4 (lib. bdg.)
[1. Mermaids—Fiction. 2. Love—Fiction.] I. Title.
PZ7 .S3787 Te 2003
[Fic]—dc21
                                                            2002010981

Typography by Amy Ryan
1 2 3 4 5 6 7 8 9 10

First Edition

To my mom,
with all my love,
for teaching me to swim

And to my brother, Mark,
for his generosity, support,
and expert advice in guiding me
through new waters

Teenage Mermaid

Spencer

I panicked. I totally freaked out! The wave crashed down over me and my surfboard. I went down, down, down. Life-giving oxygen floated out of reach, above the waters that had swallowed me.

I'm going to drown! I'm only fifteen. I haven't gotten my driver's license yet. I haven't surfed the famous Pipeline in Hawaii. I haven't fallen in love—unless my *Sports Illustrated* swimsuit poster counts.

I barely had any breath left as I desperately tried to reach the surface. Then it hit me—not the meaning of life, but my surfboard.

Time stood still. My underwater world was peaceful. I drifted helplessly like an astronaut who suddenly becomes detached from the mother ship.

People rescued from the brink of death talk about seeing a white light. Others claim to hover above their body and peacefully watch the crisis as it unfolds. But, instead, I saw her.

Maybe it's 'cause I'm a raging hormonal teenager that I had this particular vision.

Out of nowhere she appeared—golden yellow and sun-fire orange hair sparkled like tiny stars and flowed in the glistening water. The most wonderful pink-lipped smile flashed before me. Her angelic skin glowed; her piercing ocean-blue eyes stared through me and touched my soul. She floated majestically before me, a silver locket in the shape of a heart dangling from her lovely neck. This had to be a dream, or a sure sign that I had already died and gone to heaven!

I had never seen this dream girl before. She definitely didn't go to Seaside High. Nothing plastic on this girl. No silicone or liposuction marks. Just that sparkling silver heart.

Where did this angel girl come from? Why was she swimming at six o'clock in the freezing morning? Why wasn't she drowning like I was? There was no sign of a snorkel or a tank anywhere. Why did she swim like a fish? And what was that strange bikini bottom? Aquamarine metallic spandex all the way to her funky nouveau riche flipper gear.

I must have gone into shock. My underwater world started to fade dead away when she did something that was definite dream material—she kissed me. This gorgeous glistening girl! Kissed me! Not with air. Not with water. But with life. With love!

It was the best kiss of my life—and, if it was to be my last, it wasn't such a bad way to go. She took me by her soft healing hand as I struggled for life and gracefully pulled me to the surface, where I gasped a grateful gulp of California's fabulous smog. I coughed and choked, but I felt the warmth of the shimmering sun and smiled back appreciatively as she treaded water, grinning and glowing like a swimming angel.

And then everything went black.

I awoke blinded by the sun, my surfboard lying next to me, my wet suit still damp, sand clinging to my hair, the tide gently rolling over my feet.

I slowly sat up, wondering what had happened. According to my waterproof Fossil, it was nine-thirty—I was totally late for school. I had a throbbing headache. Now it all made sense. I must have been dehydrated this morning and passed out on the beach. The rest had to be a dream.

I attempted to stand, not wanting to annoy Mr. Johnson by being any later to chemistry than usual. But my palm stung. I prayed I hadn't been pricked by a jellyfish. Not only was I dehydrated, but I had been poisoned as well. I opened my clenched fist. It wasn't a wound from a man-of-war—it was a sparkling silver heart!

I apprehensively caressed the mysterious silver heart and gazed out toward the rolling sea. Maybe I had wiped out and hit my head on my surfboard. Maybe I *did* almost drown. Maybe I had been saved. And maybe in the struggle I had pulled the necklace off a—mermaid?

Maybe I was safer surfing the Internet.

Lilly

hat I did was forbidden. To see one is objectionable, to be seen is prohibited, but to touch an Earthee is punishable by exile. And I, fifteen-year-old Waterlilly, touched one on the lips!

"Waterlilly, it's your turn to give your report," Mrs. Current, our social cultures teacher, said, peering through her crystal spectacles.

My eyes were focused out the cave-room window on a school of rainbow fish as my classmates delivered boring presentations on seagulls, sea lions, sea turtles, and sea horses. I couldn't help but daydream about my terrestrial encounter with the Earthee on my way to school this morning.

Pacific Reefs, population 7,000, was a beautiful

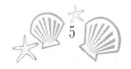

community to every inhabitant—but me. The finball stadium was the town's main attraction, obnoxiously sitting in the center of town surrounded by the police station, town council, expensive shops, and restaurants. Modest cave dwellings in neat little rows filled the outlying valley, all painted a conservative opalescent color.

Pacific Reefs High School was a massive cave with winding tunnels leading to stuffy classrooms with rock doors that shut us from the outside world and crystal clear windows that teased me to wonder what lay in the world beyond.

"Waterlilly," Mrs. Current reprimanded. "How many times do I have to call your name? It's your turn!"

I floated hesitantly before my classmates, who were attentively sitting in a semicircle, their tails draped around their rock chairs. I was wearing a radical Tidal Wavewear metallic green top with matching tail-skin. Silver sprinkles glittered in my blonde hair, which fell loosely over my shoulders. Although it was standard for a mermaid to display her hair pulled up in a twist or back in a tail, I always let mine flow with the rhythms of nature.

As I glanced up from my slate notebook, I looked at a sea of perfectly pristine mergirls who stared back with contempt. I had always been an outcast at Pacific

Reefs High, a flighty jellyfish in a school of tuna. I floated to my own wave, read banned books, arrived late to class, and wondered what lay beyond the tide.

School was a prison sentence and I had to serve three more years! I felt confined by structured time, constrained by dictated thought, restricted by an out-of-date school board, which insisted on teaching the absurd theory that Earthees were a lower life form. How could I accept this? My great-grandfather was rumored to have been an Earthee who fell in love with my mermaid great-grandma. With the help of magic, love, and a full moon, he had converted to a merman. My parents denied it ever happened.

"Complete nonsense!" my mom always said when I brought up the subject. The only reason I thought the story was true was that my mom kept an elegant silver heart in a Butterfly Venus shell in the bottom of her dresser. Great-grandpa found it in a sunken ship, or so my mother said.

"It's just an heirloom! You can have it when you are eighteen and not a day before," my mother always chided when I tried to open the shell.

Even though I didn't know great-grandpa, he was my hero. Living in the Pacific was confining enough to this teenage mermaid. Fashions were claustrophobic, laws were so three decades ago. And true love seemed as far away as the moon!

I always wondered what lay beyond the sea. Were Earthteens bored? Did they stare out into a sea of look-alikes when they gave reports at school? Did they feel like outcasts ostracized by other Earthteens? Did human prejudices against other humans exist?

Mrs. Current called on me.

"Earthees," I began, reading from my notebook.

"Earthees?" Mrs. Current barked. "They aren't an acceptable subject. The assignment was sea creatures!"

I heard some giggling and snickering. We merpeople keep to ourselves, afraid of swimming out of our watery limits. Although we studied Earth history and knew Earth languages, which our scholars had deciphered from books and letters in sunken vessels, it was not done out of interest, but for our survival. Earthees catch fish for sport! Imagine if they hooked us? We needed to be a stroke ahead of their game. No explorers with the National Earth Administration who'd adventured to Earth had ever returned. All that remained from their failed missions was fear. We got our information from litter thrown into our sea and explorers who peered through periscopes hidden behind rocks. A small and closed community were we, wanting nothing to threaten our social order.

"Earthees," I began again, "are indigenous to land. Like merpeople, they are mammals, but breathe air

instead of water. Their movements are propelled by legs instead of a tail and fin," I said to a sea of glazed eyes.

It was as if I were talking about slimy squid. Merpeople are no more interested in humans than whales are interested in the fish that eat the fungus that grows on their backs. Earthees are considered just a step above squid. And just like the squid, no one is going to invite them over for dinner!

"Your attendance is already poor and your grades are sinking. And now you offer this as your project?" Mrs. Current sneered.

"But I put a lot of time into this," I pleaded. The room was silent as the students and I waited for her verdict.

"Go ahead," she said, sighing, bubbles spewing out of her mouth, "but your grade will reflect the lack of adherence to the assignment."

"Earthees have learned to swim," I offered, knowing that I was treading in chilly arctic waters. "They've built ships that can carry schools of them from one place to another for travel or battle. They are very intelligent."

"They don't believe in our existence, do they?" Mrs. Current interrupted.

"Well, in my research . . . no."

"Then how intelligent can they really be?" Mrs.

Current said snidely, tapping her stick on her polished coral desk.

"They fight gravity by balancing on boards on rising waves. They also use covered boats with wheels to drive on land."

Mrs. Current let out a yawn so audible merpeople in the Caspian Sea could have heard.

"They've figured out how to fly," I argued.

"So have seagulls," Mrs. Current said. "But I wouldn't marry one."

The whole class laughed. I took a deep breath.

"We know all this. Tell us something we've never heard," Mrs. Current challenged.

She was right. I wasn't reporting anything we didn't already know, anything we hadn't studied in Earth history class.

"I will," I said brightly, suddenly remembering my necklace. The story of my Earthee great-grandfather would surely mesmerize them. I proudly reached for the silver heart around my neck. But I only felt flesh!

Gone? How could it be gone? My mother will kill me! I had placed it around my neck just this morning before school. I had it on when I left home and as I . . . Oh, no! Earthdude must have pulled it off when I saved him.

"Well?" Mrs. Current asked impatiently.

I was powerless now. My audience was hypnotized

by boredom. The necklace, like my classmates' attention, was miles away.

"So, you've never actually observed an Earthee up close," Mrs. Current said. "One in the flesh. One with real legs. One that was breathing."

The class sat up. I could feel the undercurrent pushing against me, as I resisted its force.

Forget the necklace! I would tell her exactly how Earthees kiss, and knock the shriveled condescending merhag out of the ocean and up to the moon! But I knew what I had done was scandalous. I hadn't observed an Earthee with a periscope, I had kissed one.

The class studied me, suddenly interested, curious, repulsed, waiting for my response.

"Well, if you must know . . ." I smiled defiantly. "Just this morning—"

Suddenly flashlight fish signaled the end of class. Like a lucky trout, I was off the hook.

"Chain me with seaweed if you must, but I'd do it again in a minute!" I proudly confessed to my supercelestial best friend, Waverly, as we sat on our assigned seats in Pacific history class later that day.

We were inseparable, Wave and I, despite our differences. She was dark as the deepest part of the ocean, while I was as pasty pale as white coral. She

arrived for predators and prey class early; I was lucky to arrive at all. She was right of the shoreline, while I was radically left. But years ago she'd politely taken me under her wing like a seagull helping a misguided chick. She tried to point me in the right direction, persuade me to swim within the lines. She didn't care if my great-grandfather was a converted Earthee. She followed the rules and tried to keep me from rewriting them.

I immediately burst with all the details of my Earthly adventure.

"Waterlilly, would you like to share your secret with me after school today?" Mr. Dorsal suddenly scolded, floating above Wave and me like a circling shark, as we scrawled out "Pacific Settlers" essays on flattened petrified driftwood.

"I'm sorry," I said to appease him. The thinly mustached teacher glared down at me, then quickly floated to the front of the class to carve onto the lesson stone, which rested on a blue coral easel.

Waverly and I were silent for about a minute. Then it was gossip as usual.

"You're swimming with danger!" Wave whispered nervously, fingering her shell-beaded braids.

"I overslept and was heading for school when I saw him drop down," I exclaimed under my breath. "The

poor guy, he just couldn't handle the sea."

"Earthees can't really, can they?" Waverly chided. "They pretend to, with their motorboats and jet skis, always upsetting the natural rhythms of the water."

"But this guy didn't have a motor," I defended. "He had a flashy yellow seaboard. And it hit him right in the head!"

"Serves him right." Wave laughed.

"His eyes bulged when he saw me—like he was seeing a shipwrecked ghost!" I continued.

"You know what Earthees do to dolphins and whales, Lilly. They trap them in nets, spear them, and pluck them from the sea. Earthees spill sticky oil into our environment. Think what he could have done to you. You could have been harpooned like a whale."

"But I had to help him!"

"Only you would rescue an Earthee! No other mermaid would have gone near him. You'll get into major trouble if anyone finds out. Your parents would send you to the Atlantic."

Wave was right. The Atlantic was oceans away! Cold, lonely, the boarding-school capital of the sea. My overbearing parents were already frustrated enough with my rebelliousness. Saving an Earthee was equivalent to a one-way ticket on Eastern Whale Express Lines.

13

But then Wave suddenly changed her tone. "What was it like?" she asked, like a gossip reporter for the *Intercoastal Starfish*.

"He actually tasted sweet. Much sweeter than I would have imagined. Like a caramelized sea nettle," I recalled, licking my lips. "He has the kind of soul you can feel with your own! Not like a typical mer-dude whose goal is to drink Shark Attacks and watch professional finball."

"Was he hot?"

"Scorching! He had deep-red clay-colored hair, a chiseled jaw, and soft melt-worthy lips. He really needed me, Wave. I've never felt that before. When I helped him breathe, he came alive like magic. His smile even made the water sparkle!"

"Are you positive no one saw you?" Waverly warned.

"Not a soul on land or sea," I assured Waverly. "Not even when I pushed his yellow seaboard onto the sand. It's a good thing we've been taking aqua-aerobics. That thing was heavy!"

"Do you think he knows where we live?" she worried.

"He was out of it anyway. Besides, Earthees are supposed to be stupid mammals. The encyclopedia said they believe Loch Ness is full of monsters."

"And that Bermuda has a mysterious triangle!" she added, giggling.

"But Wave, this is our secret," I demanded, suddenly serious, holding out my pinky finger. "Promise?"

"I promise," she said reluctantly, clasping my finger in her own.

"Now that you've sworn, I have a final confession!"

"Don't tell me you're in love!" she said, rolling her eyes.

"I—"

"No more talking!" Mr. Dorsal reprimanded.

I couldn't pay attention to the lesson Mr. Dorsal was carving on the black stone. I daydreamed about my encounter with Earthdude. The closest I'd ever been to seeing an Earthee before was secretly watching them swim, surf, and sail, from my hangout by the rocks by the pier.

As Wave and I swam to our next class I crashed into a teen titan in the crowded tunnel. It was Beach.

"Imagine you two bumping into each other," Wave said dramatically, stopping beside us. Classmates continued to swim all around us—above and below. Wave gave a flirty wave to her boyfriend, Tide, who was kicking a finball through the crowd below us.

15

Both merdudes were scorchers—the best finball players in school. Tide had black hair and midnight skin like Wave's. His biceps rippled and his stomach was strong, lean, and showed off every muscle. Beach was the white coral version of Tide with pale skin and spiky white hair. Tide wore a red tank top and black tail-skin, while Beach had a deep-blue tank and black tail-skin.

Beach had just dumped Misty, the varsity pep-squad captain, when he found her at Club Atlantis without him. Wave was ready to fill the vacancy with me, whether I liked it or not!

Beach looked down with his glistening blue eyes. His sun-white hair poked out all over his head like a sea cactus. He was a typical sleek shark—smooth, leering, checking out his prey until he was ready to pounce.

"We'll be at Shipwreck after school," Beach said, gently stroking my hair. "You'll be there?"

"I have homework," I said, pushing his hand away.

"You never do your homework," Wave whispered, glaring at me.

"Tonight I have a big assignment," I declared.

Beach might be perfect for a girl who wanted to cheer her boyfriend on from the sidelines. But I didn't want a boyfriend that wanted to wear me like a new finball jersey. I wanted someone truly special, some-

one whose soul was reflected in my own. I wanted to be in love.

"We'll be there!" Wave said with a smile as the two titans swam off to class.

"I have to study for my marine biology exam," I lied.

"Tomorrow," Wave insisted. "Today you have to study boyfriend biology," and she dragged me off to lunch.

Spencer

An *under*water kiss?" Chainsaw asked skeptically at our lockers. It was after second bell in the crowded hallway. Chainsaw, my best friend and worst enemy, was born wearing braces, and, man, those things could cut through steel! "What girl has ever kissed you out of the water?" he ribbed me.

"Shhh!" I whispered.

I didn't want my romantic rescue to flash all over school. I'm a fringe guy, even more unpopular than Chainsaw, content simply not to end up trapped inside a senior's locker. On a scale of one to ten, I give myself a seven and a half in looks, but I get extra points for personality, which, unfortunately, most people have never seen. And did I mention I'm smart?

Not smart enough to be a geek, thank goodness. But I do maintain a B-plus average, which is pretty good for someone who never raises his hand in class. And I know the entire script of *The Godfather*.

"Maybe it was just a dream!" Chainsaw said, and laughed.

I rolled my eyes, pulling my European history textbook from my locker and stuffing it into my backpack.

"And you didn't touch her?" he went on in typical Chainsaw fashion.

"I was drowning, dude!"

"A gorgeous babe kisses you and you don't make a move?" he asked in hormonal disbelief.

"I thought I was going to die! What part aren't you getting?"

"Dude . . . did you at least get her number?"

"You don't get it—I've never seen anything like her before," I confessed.

"Even in my dreams, I always get the number," Chainsaw said, slamming his locker shut. "Keep dreaming, Stone," he added, sauntering off.

"I got this instead!" I said, catching up and proudly dangling the necklace in front of him. "Anyone can get a phone number!"

His eyes were momentarily mesmerized by the swinging silver heart.

"She kissed you, saved your life, and gave you a necklace?" he asked skeptically.

"Well she didn't exactly give it to me."

Chain scrutinized the necklace like a pawnbroker. "Not bad, Stone," he said, hitting me in the arm. "Not bad at all."

My cousin Dennis spotted the love of his life on the crowded New Jersey turnpike and engaged her in conversation. When the traffic moved and she changed lanes he realized he hadn't gotten her number. So he bought a billboard on that same stretch of highway. Now they have three kids.

But I wasn't destined to find my true love via a giant billboard, the newspaper, or the Internet. *I* had to go to the sea.

I wrote my message on a library computer during third bell study hall, and then Xeroxed it on sheets of yellow, pink, red, and turquoise paper. I was temporarily blinded by the continuous flash from the copier when I heard a screeching voice exclaim, "You're using up all my paper!"

Mrs. Barney, our toothpick-thin librarian, reached for the paper tray. "'Single White Male'," she read. "This looks like a personal ad!" she exclaimed, her forehead wrinkling.

I quickly grabbed the paper from her hand and

snatched the remaining stack from the paper tray. "I'm doing a report on relationships!"

"All these copies for one report?" she said, scrunching her witchlike nose.

"Did I say report?" I stammered. "I meant . . . collage. For art."

"Personal ads," she said. "I remember when all one had to do was go to the disco."

I almost cracked at the thought of Mrs. Barney groovin' with a John Travolta look-alike.

"I can't imagine a world where love is so impersonal. There was nothing more personal than a man in tight pants spinning a girl around a room all night," she said, gazing out the window at the ocean far below. "But don't let me get you down," she added, placing her hand on my shoulder. "Everyone finds their true love, if they want to."

"I'm hoping to meet mine at the south goalpost!" I said, stuffing the ads in my backpack, and bolting from the library.

Chainsaw and I snuck off school property during lunch and raced down the hill to the beach, where we plastered the pier with my ad. We even tacked sheets to an empty lifeguard stand. By the time we were finished, the beachfront looked like Times Square on New Year's Day. Exhausted, Chainsaw and I made our way back up to school just in time for English lit.

The message read: "SWM, 15, seeking golden-haired beauty who saved my life. I wear your silver heart close to my own. Meet me at Seaside High Stadium (south goalpost) at 8:30 A.M. I want to thank you."

I didn't put down my name, phone number, or e-mail address, to avoid hassles from the local graffiti police, and to weed out any desperate forty-year-old women with amorous intentions!

Lilly

fter school I dragged Waverly to the rocks underneath the pier where we sat out of human sight, our tails safely hidden in the water. "That's what you've been waiting all day to tell me? That Earthdude has your great-grandfather's necklace? Your mom will kill you!" Waverly shrieked.

Luckily, there wasn't much activity on the beachfront today. Just an orange-vested man taking down brightly colored sheets hanging all over the pier. Of course it's dangerous to approach land, but at the moment I was more worried about being near my mother. I had to figure out a solution—and fast. Merpeople can only inhale air for about ten minutes before having to return underwater.

23

"I'm going!" Wave said impatiently. "We can talk about this dilemma in your hideaway, where it's safe."

"I need help, now," I said, grabbing her arm. "I wanted to use the necklace for my Earthee project. I was going to return it right after school. Mom never would have known it was gone!"

"So Earthdude grabbed it in the struggle for his life?" Wave realized, shaking her head in disapproval.

"I have to find that heart immediately! If Mom opens her Butterfly Venus shell—"

Wave gasped, pulling at her hair in disgust. "A seagull pooped on me!"

"No, it's just a piece of paper," I said, and laughed, grabbing it before it blew away. Crisp letters written in black ink smeared onto my wet hand. "'SWM,'" I read slowly.

"Let's go before someone sees us!" Wave said anxiously.

"'Fifteen . . .'" I continued. "'Seeking golden-haired beauty.'" I gazed up at Waverly. "My hair is golden."

"So it is, but it'll turn blue if we don't return underwater!"

She inched away from me but I quickly grabbed her arm.

"'Who saved my life.' How poetic!" I said dreamily, gazing at the cloud-filled sky.

"'Who saved my life?'" Wave repeated, suddenly

intrigued. She grabbed the paper. "This is totally cosmic! 'I wear your silver heart close to my own.'"

Our eyes locked in disbelief.

"Silver heart?" Wave repeated, incredulous.

"Saved his life . . ."

"Golden hair? Lilly, it's a message from that Earthdude! He's trying to find you!"

"It couldn't be . . . that's impossible," I said, bewildered.

"This is *way* dangerous," Wave argued.

"It's totally glacial! Read the rest—I'm too freaked out!"

"'Meet me at Seaside High Stadium (south goalpost) at 8:30 A.M. I want to thank you,'" she read.

"Thank me?" I asked, grabbing the parchment. Had my Earthdude written this?

"Don't even think about it! We never saw this paper," Waverly urged, grabbing the note and tossing it into the sea.

My heart fell as the pink paper gently floated away from us on the ocean's surface. It drifted out of sight on a cresting wave.

I could tell my mom I took her locket to school without her permission and lost it, and she would immediately sell my precious dolphin, Bubbles. Or I could tell her the truth, that my lips were pressed against a forbidden Earthee and he yanked it off in

that life-giving kiss. In which case, she'd sell me.

My options were clear. I had to get the necklace back.

"It's either a day at Seaside High or an eternity in an Atlantic boarding school," I concluded, and we dove back into the water.

Wave and I rode Bubbles, my dolphin, to the Underworld far below the reef's warm water and bright colors. The water in the Underworld was frigid and the only colors that could be seen even with our sharp mermaid eyes were indigo and purple. To get there we had to ride past the finball stadium, past the school, past the recycling center, and dive down into a steep, jagged valley with giant stingrays swarming around. We'd never been this far from home before.

"I don't think this is a good idea," Wave said, sitting behind me, tugging my hair.

Bubbles, too, was reluctant to press on and I had to tap her reassuringly to dive deeper.

"It's so arctic!" Wave cried through chattering teeth as we sped to lower depths.

"Don't be such a jellyfish! We'll be there soon!"

"That's what I'm afraid of! If those tiger sharks don't kill us, our parents will."

Just then I, too, noticed several tiger sharks swarming over a mangled tuna below us.

26

"Hurry! Hurry!" Wave shrieked in horror.

"Relax, they've already found lunch," I said, steering Bubbles around the feeding predators.

"Yeah, but we're dessert," Wave yelled, as the biggest shark broke away from the rest. "They've spotted us!"

Suddenly our lives were in major danger!

Pacific Reef had shark fences that repelled sharks from invading our city, but every once in a while one got through and caused panic. Only last year a merman was attacked on his way to a finball game. We usually carried shark mace in our purses, but I had foolishly taken mine out earlier to make room for my crystal sea horse collection which I intended to barter in the Underworld.

The biggest shark was fast approaching and Bubbles was whining anxiously. I tapped her hurriedly. "Go, baby, go!"

"Lilly, use your mace!" Wave shrieked.

"Mine's at home—use yours!"

"Home? What good's it doing at home?" She scrambled through her pink backpack as the shark drew closer. "I can't find it!"

"Look harder," I shouted.

"Here's my compact! My comb!"

"Today, Waverly! Today!"

"My lobster sandwich from lunch . . . here it is!"

27

But in her panic the mace slipped from her hand and sank to the ocean floor.

I think even Bubbles let out a shriek.

The shark was now just yards away, his gray eyes piercing us and his jaws open, waiting for a triple-decker treat.

"Help!" Wave called desperately. "Help! Someone help us!"

"The sandwich! That's why he's following us—he smells dead fish," I screamed.

"Soon he's going to smell dead mermaids!" Wave screamed, squeezing my waist.

"Throw him the sandwich!" I commanded.

But Wave just grabbed me harder.

I peeled the sandwich from Waverly's paralyzed hands and turned Bubbles around sharply. The shark, rising to attack us, opened his jaws again and I threw the lobster sandwich as hard as I could into his mouth. The shark seemed bewildered for a moment, then suddenly pleased, and swam past so closely I could have reached out and touched his belly.

"We're alive!" Waverly laughed, waving her arms.

"That was electric!" I exclaimed.

Even Bubbles smiled brightly.

"Now let's go home," Waverly said.

"But we're almost there."

"Are you crazy?" she asked, out of breath.

I tapped Bubbles onward and within minutes we dove as debris and litter floated past us into a darkened filthy district where homeless merpeople begged for coins, addicts scored stingray venom, and dancing merladies hung behind glass-enclosed caves enticing mermen into their lairs.

I secured Bubbles to a rock outside Hurricane's House of Tattoos. "We'll just be a minute," I said, petting his nose as he squirmed nervously.

A one-eyed merman who stunk of fermented jellyfish leered at us from the alley. "Hey, girls!"

I grabbed Wave's trembling arm and swam past him. We'd heard of Madame Pearl from kids at school. Some said she was a sea witch, some said she was a charlatan, but she was my only hope.

MADAME PEARL'S POTION PALACE. The painted clay letters were weathered and cracked, but the store was smaller and less frightening than I had imagined. No snakes or eels, no shrunken skulls hanging in the windows. Just a small, dilapidated cave with seaweed curtains swaying with the undercurrent.

We opened the barnacle-encrusted front door and cautiously entered. A woman loomed over us whose crinkly face showed the signs of someone who'd been in the lower depths for decades. Her porcelain flesh was puffed out like a blowfish, and her chest spilled over her huge black sequined shirt.

"Madame Pearl?" I asked hesitantly.

She quickly sized us up with her skeptical gaze. "This isn't the place for two young mermaids," she said.

"I need your help."

She grabbed my small hand in her large one and closed the door behind us. She led us into a consultation room with a heavy round table and chairs dripping with black lace. "You have come to hear your destiny," she said when we were seated.

"Well, not exactly," I answered.

"You want to know if your current relationship is a lasting one?"

"I'm afraid not."

"You want me to tell you about your past lives?"

"No!"

"Well, tell me already! I'm not a psychic!" she blurted out.

"You're not?" Wave asked.

"I need a potion," I whispered.

"You can get potions anywhere these days. Kids sell that stuff in school bathrooms. They've plumb run me out of business," she said, rising. "You shouldn't risk your lives to come here for that. I can't be bothered with such things anymore!"

She floated through a thick seaweed curtain into another room.

30

"But I want a special one!" I said, following her, but the seaweed curtain closed in my face. Wave swam over, looking relieved. "We better take off."

"I don't know where else to go!" I called through the curtain.

There was no response. "Let's leave," Wave whispered, tugging at my arm.

"Only magic can help me!" I exclaimed, not moving.

I could hear the faint wailing of a beggar blowing bubbles through a cone shell outside. There was no response from Madame Pearl.

I opened the front door, resigned to leave, when suddenly the curtains opened and Madame Pearl peeked her head through. "Magic?" she inquired. "No one's asked me for magic for years! Everyone wants youth potions, aphrodisiacs, or cold relief. Sit down!"

She drew the curtains over the windows and returned to the table.

"Now, what kind of magic do you need? Longer hair? A spell cast upon an enemy?"

"I want to be an Earthee!"

Her jaw dropped. She got up from the table. "Out of the question!"

"But I'll be sent to the Atlantic!"

"That potion is of much greater danger than banishment to the Atlantic!"

"I'm willing to take the risk!"

"And why, may I ask, are you willing to risk your life for a few hours on land?"

"I have to get my great-grandfather's necklace back!"

"A necklace? Buy another!"

"You don't understand. It's priceless. And I know where it is. It won't take me an hour."

"But there are consequences. If you stay past the rising moon, you'll lose your mermaid form forever."

"I'll only be on land for a few minutes."

Madame Pearl fingered her crystal necklace. "I will need parental consent," she said, rising, and rummaging through a box of forms.

I opened my purse and spilled out my crystal sea horse collection, which slowly sank onto the table.

Madame Pearl stared at the crystal almost salivating, as if I had put a marinated lobster tail in front of her.

"These are yours?" she asked skeptically, forgetting the box of forms.

"It took me six years to collect all of them."

"Wait here a minute," she said, scooping the sea horses into the top layer of her black skirt. She quickly left the room. The seaweed curtain, slightly opened, revealed her working fervently on the other side. Wave and I peeked through.

Madame Pearl floated high in a cluttered kitchen. Bottles with sea creatures and hardened seaweed books lined the marble shelves. Purple crystals hung from the stalactites on the ceiling. She grabbed a book from the top shelf and set it open on a wooden table. Then she began adding ingredients from labeled shells: an octopus leg, the eye of a shrimp, the tongue of a frog. She placed them and a dash of herbs in a green glass bottle, closed it with a cork and vigorously shook the concoction. Finally she held the bottle to her chest and spoke words I couldn't understand.

When she looked up, Wave and I quickly floated back to our chairs.

Madame Pearl returned. The gook-filled bottle leaked the most horrible smell.

"You must drink the entire potion within three hours from now. Not a minute after, or it will lose its potency," she declared, handing it to me.

"Can't I just place it under my pillow?" I asked, holding the bottle at arm's length.

"I knew this was a mistake," she said, extending her hand to take the potion back.

"I'll do it!" I vowed, pulling the bottle close to my heart.

"You'll have until moonrise to return to the ocean. Not a second longer!" she warned.

"No one will even miss me," I said, getting up.

"Not a second longer!" she threatened, when I opened the front door.

"Or I'll turn into a sea fairy and grow wings?" I teased.

"Or you'll turn into an Earthee—forever!"

"Forever?" Waverly asked, grabbing my arm.

"Forever," Madame Pearl repeated, with terror in her midnight eyes. "You will forget how to breathe underwater. You will plummet to the ocean floor and drown!"

"Drown?" I said, shocked. "Impossible."

"Drown!" Wave echoed. "I told you this wasn't a good idea."

"I'll only be an hour. Anyway, there's always a way to reverse spells," I said.

"There's a legend that one can be saved through a kiss of love from an Earthee, who would then change into a merperson. But that's only a legend," Madame Pearl said.

"I don't need to worry about drowning, about love, or the moonrise. I'll be home before the tide comes in."

"Remember the rules, child," she warned as we left. "This isn't breaking a curfew—this is changing your destiny!"

I placed the horrible-smelling mixture in my abalone purse, unleashed Bubbles, and Wave and I raced away as mermen howled from the depths.

Spencer

I was too impatient to wait for tomorrow. After school Chainsaw agreed to comb the beach with me in search of my personal lifesaver. He wasn't hard to convince. Looking for a beautiful girl? He did that every day of his life. Chainsaw had braces, freckles, and straw hair, but that didn't stop him from thinking he was a studly gift to the female gender.

When we reached the beach I was mortified. All my ads were gone. Didn't law enforcement have better things to do? How would I ever find her now?

"Cheer up! There's a lot of other girls here!" Chain said happily. "Look at those two over there," he said, pointing to a blonde and redhead lying on towels. He fearlessly walked over to them. "Hey, ladies," he said gallantly to the two bikini-clad girls. "My friend, Spencer," Chainsaw said, "was knocked out by his surfboard this morning and nearly drowned. He was saved by an intelligent, pretty girl. He's looking for his rescuer to give her a sizeable reward."

The bleached-blonde girl didn't have time for Chainsaw's charm and placed her headphones back over her ears. But the redhead giggled, intrigued by this new pick-up line.

"And you were wondering whether it was me or my friend?" she asked, taking a swig of Evian.

"Exactly," Chain said. "You see, Spencer was a breath away from death and his vision was understandably blurry. The only way he can identify his life-saver is if she performs mouth-to-mouth again."

The girl laughed wildly. "Did you ever hear that one before?" she said to her friend. "I told you Californians were wild!"

The redhead looked me over as if I were a giant ice cream cone, contemplating if I were worth the calories.

"Let's go," I said, nudging Chainsaw.

"Well, what's the reward?" she suddenly asked. "I mean if I'm the one—"

"This necklace," Chainsaw added, pointing to the heart dangling from my neck.

"Are you crazy?" I whispered, glaring.

"That's an antique, isn't it?" she said, eyeing the

sparkling heart. She smiled at me and rose to her feet.

"What are you doing?" her friend asked, taking off her headphones and sitting up.

"We came to California to have fun, didn't we?" the redhead asked, adjusting her blue bikini bottom. "Stuff like this never happens in Wisconsin!"

She stood face to face with me. I wasn't sure if she was going to kiss me or laugh at me. Her red lipstick was faded from the sun and her sweet chubby cheeks were shiny from sunscreen. Three days ago I would have jumped at the chance to kiss an attractive older girl. I would have even kissed Arnold Schwarzenegger in a blue bikini. But that life-saving kiss had changed me. The flirty tourist smiled, giggled, and stared into my eyes, ignoring her friend, who was shaking her head.

What was happening? Girls never fall for this stuff!

"Okay, pretend you're drowning," she giggled, leaning in.

And I did something I never in my testosterone-driven years thought I'd do. I extended my arm to her shoulders, blocking her from kissing me.

"Are you crazy?" Chainsaw screamed.

"I'm sorry, you're not her," I apologized, and walked away.

Chain stepped in. "You can save me!" he pleaded, leaning in to her.

"Sorry," she quipped, pointing to his braces, "I'm not into heavy metal!"

"Are you out of your mind?" Chain panted, catching up to me.

"You don't get it. This isn't about scoring!" I said, turning around. "Promise me you'll really help me find her!"

"Okay, okay. If you promise me one thing."

"Yes?"

"Next time I get to be the one who was rescued!"

I leaned against the railing on the pier, frustrated and exhausted, staring at the waves crashing against the rocks.

"Dude, like if she's that beautiful," Chainsaw said, "she's gotta have a major boyfriend. Probably three of them."

"Thanks for the support."

"I'm trying to protect you."

"Protect me from what?"

"Maybe there's a reason you haven't seen this dream girl. She could be married. She could have escaped from prison."

"You just can't believe a beautiful girl would like me!"

"Of course I believe it, man! You're a surfer stud! That buff babe was ready to smack your lips and she didn't even know you, the true you. The you that'll turn in early because you have to surf the next day. The you that reads *Romeo and Juliet* because you want to. The you that'll hang out with scum like me!"

I couldn't help but smile. Chainsaw seemed to be out for himself, but in the end he was always there for me. "I just want this dream girl to be major league. I don't want to lose you to a flaky heartbreaker," he said.

"You won't lose me," I replied, playfully punching him in the arm.

"Come on," he said, setting his chewing gum on the railing and then flicking it into the waves. "Let's play a couple games of Alien Attack at my house."

"No thanks," I said, as we began walking back to the beach. "I don't feel like vaporizing green creatures."

"Don't feel like zapping aliens?" Chainsaw said, stopping in his tracks. "Damn! I've already lost you!"

Lilly

We took a detour home from Madame Pearl's just in case the sharks were still feeding. To our immense relief we encountered nothing more dangerous on our way back to civilization than a moray eel; that is, until we reached Shipwreck, a restaurant popular with the teen finball crowd, where an equally dangerous school of sharks ambushed us— Beach and Tide!

"Perfect timing!" Wave said, jumping off Bubbles and tying her leash to coral.

"I have to take my potion," I whispered adamantly. "I can't stay!"

"Sure you can," Beach said, grabbing my hand and helping me off.

"I said I have to go!" I exclaimed, trying to unleash Bubbles.

"It's party time, urchin baby," Beach said, bumping into me and accidentally knocking my purse into the sea.

"My purse!" I screamed, darting after my precious potion as it floated away. Beach beat me to it and started for the door.

"I need that!" I hollered.

"Why? Are you paying? I like a woman who's in charge!" And he disappeared into the restaurant.

I followed after him through a massive hole in the hull which had caused the ship to sink. The interior was decorated with red vinyl chairs and silver metal tables, and strings of glow fish and fluorescent lights draped the ceiling. Waitresses wore white sailor hats and navy ties.

"Beach's birthday party is tomorrow," Wave said, grabbing my arm and plopping me down beside him.

I grabbed my purse back.

"You'll be there?" Beach asked, nudging me.

"Of course she will," Wave answered, cuddling next to Tide.

"My mom needs me at home," I announced.

The waitress brought an appetizer of candied mussels and asked for our drink orders.

"Frog juice," Wave said. "Since when do you listen

to your mother?" she challenged me.

"We're having company," I said.

"Make that two frog juices!" Wave ordered.

I gazed out the porthole at Bubbles, reluctantly leashed to the pole. Like her, I couldn't break free.

Wave tied her backpack to her chair so it wouldn't float away, but I desperately clung to my purse. She was cuddling with Tide; Beach was almost sitting on my lap. I wondered where Earthdude was. *I wear your silver heart close to my own.* Was he wearing it right now? I stared at my watch.

"It's been lovely, but I have tons of homework," I said, rising.

"Bored already?" Beach asked. "Let's bop!"

He grabbed my arm, dropped a half-eaten mussel back in the shell basket and pulled me to the dance floor at the stern of the ship. Music was piped in through sponge speakers that hung from the ship's walls. A wave machine gently undulated to the rhythm of the dance floor water, making couples rock into each other. Twirling lasers flashed red sharks, yellow sea horses, and purple hearts. Couples jammed above and below us, working off the worries of a bad-hair day. My purse dangled helplessly as Beach spun me around.

"You're a great dancer!" Beach smiled, as a couple suddenly did a wild corkscrew spin over our heads, almost crashing into us. "I bet that's not all you're

good at," he said, pulling me close. He leaned in and kissed me.

Beach kissing me? He was tasty, but something was missing in his kiss. Love?

And that wasn't all that was missing. I pushed him away and reached for my abalone purse. But it wasn't on my shoulder!

"My purse! My purse! It's gone!" I shouted.

"It's okay. I'm paying!"

Suddenly the water felt as thick as mud. I was moving in slow motion as I pushed through the sea of dancers. I swam toward the ceiling, dove back to the floor. I shouted to the DJ, but he just shook his head. I scoured every table on the way back to Wave and Tide.

"Wave, I lost my purse!" I panicked.

"Aren't the Mud Rakers totally glacial?" she said, bopping her head and sipping her imported frog juice.

"My purse! It has my new purchase!" I shouted to her.

"We'll get you another," she said, almost relieved.

"Someone might mistake my medicine for a Shark Attack and wake up with two legs!" I said, glaring at her.

"Oh!" she exclaimed.

Wave, Tide, Beach, and I went off in separate directions: Beach back to the dance floor, Wave to the

bathroom, Tide to the galley, and I went to the upper deck. It felt like forever as I swam up the staircases and peered over railings, wondering if my purse had floated outside.

Deflated, I swam back to our table. My search party wasn't anywhere in sight. Had I lost them, too?

"Is this it?" Tide called, hanging at the hostess counter, holding my abalone treasure.

I swam over to him, relieved. But it felt lighter. I quickly opened it. It was empty!

My heart sank. Even Wave looked frazzled when she returned from her search.

"Oh, no!" she shouted, pointing to a preteen mer-scout sitting at a table with his troops, about to open the cork from my bottle. He leaned his head back, ready to gulp the potion down his throat.

"You're too young for this!" I said, grabbing it out of his hand.

"I didn't know! Don't tell our troop leader! Okay?" he begged.

I held the bottle tightly to my chest and made my getaway through the ship's hole.

"Wait for me!" Wave said, climbing onto Bubbles.

"So I'll see you tomorrow night at my party?" Beach called.

"She wouldn't miss it for the world," Wave answered as we sped away.

44

✰ ✰ ✰

We raced to my favorite underwater hideout—an abandoned cave not far from my home. I had fixed it up with sea lettuce curtains, portraits of Earthees I had found at an open-water market, and hot-pink clay chairs. Shelves were adorned with rusty Earthee coins, a bright orange Earthee diving fin, a black high-heeled shoe, a Beatles' *Abbey Road* compact disc, Panasonic batteries, and a carving of my parents at their wedding, dressed in white, kissing beneath a water lily patch. I used my hideout to listen to music, read teen mags, or fantasize about an Earthee life when I wanted to be alone. Only Wave knew of its existence.

"Here goes!" I said, eyeing the potion.

"Why don't you just hang it on the wall with your other treasures," Wave suggested.

"I don't have a choice," I said, trying to pry the cork off.

Wave urgently stopped my hand. "What happens if Madame Pearl is wrong? What happens if you grow two heads instead of two legs?"

"Then I'll be that much smarter!"

"You don't know what that stuff can do. You could grow two fins!" she said, pulling it back.

"Then I'll join the sea circus," I said, pulling it toward me.

"You could die!" she exclaimed. "Lilly, you could die!"

We stared at each other. Her angry eyes turned sad.

I had never really thought of that. I guess it was my nature. Act now, think later. Talk back to my parents—think about it in my room. Cut class—reflect in my hideout. Save an Earthee now—consider the consequences later. Maybe this was one time I should think before I acted.

"I won't let you die!" Wave said, jerking the bottle toward her. But suddenly the old glass bottle broke— the jagged bottom remained clenched in my hand while Wave held the broken neck. Its obnoxious contents oozed into the sea. We were both shocked, as the brown liquid slowly floated before our eyes.

There was only one thing to do. I swam after the potion and swallowed as much as I could before it diluted completely. It tasted as disgusting as it looked and it took all my effort to keep it down.

"No!" Wave shrieked, yanking me away from the potion as I struggled to cup more into my mouth.

"Let go!" I cried.

I continued swallowing the potion until I could see or smell no more.

As I wiped gooey droplets from my mouth, I fell into a coughing fit.

"Are you okay?" she cried. "I'll call a doctor!"

"No—" I said, through coughs. "I'm all right."

The sludge left a muddy tingling sensation in my

mouth and throat, all the way to my stomach, which felt like I'd eaten rotten snails. We hung, motionless, like two stingrays, waiting for the metamorphosis. Would the transformation be instant? Would it take days? I didn't know.

I stared up at the clock. Seconds became minutes. I finally sat down. The tension was too great and I pulled out *MerMusic* magazine and flipped through the pages. I scrubbed my teeth in the bathroom. I straightened my battery collection. Wave sat on a wooden Earthee chair chewing her nails.

"Look, I'm still a mermaid!" I exclaimed an hour later. "Satisfied?"

"I knew that old woman was a crackpot!" Wave sighed, hugging me. "How could we be friends if you didn't live in the water anymore?"

"I gave away my crystal collection! I could have bought front row tickets to the Psychedelic Sponges concert."

"Or a backstage pass and autographed picture," she teased.

"I'm going back tomorrow to demand a refund."

"Think of it as a lesson," she tried to comfort. "Mermaids belong in the ocean."

"And charlatans belong in the Underworld. Oh . . . I don't feel so well," I moaned, as we rode Bubbles back to my house.

Spencer

At home later that day, I couldn't concentrate on my Surf Slam 3000 video game. I gazed at my *Sports Illustrated* swimsuit poster, then tore it from my wall. Who needed a supermodel to pine over? That was kid stuff! After all, magazine girls required hours of professional makeup and pea-sized dinners. I had something real, even if it had only lasted a moment, a magical kiss from a dream girl I'd probably never see again. I switched off my desk lamp and lay on my bed, wondering if she'd ever find the ad, ever show up at the football field, if I'd ever see her again. I reflected on her pink lips, her sparkling smile, and caressed the necklace in my hand, wishing it were her.

Lilly

I lay awake in bed that night, despite being exhausted from the day's events. My round mattress hung by red vines from the ceiling, which was plastered with glow-in-the-dark suction-cupped starfish, while real sea horses swam on top of my flashy red dresser, grabbing onto the marble cone drawer handles when they wanted to rest. Banned books were stashed under my clothes in a drawer. Beneath my bed, Bubbles slept restlessly as if she'd swallowed the potion, too.

I lay awake wondering about Earth life. We knew that Earthees had legs, and we had fins. Similar, but different. But how different could they be, really, on the inside?

Above my bedroom, above Pacific Reefs, far above the surface of the water, the crescent moon shone two hundred thousand miles away in the starry sky. But I still had fins, just like all my friends who'd drunk Shark Attacks or frog juice tonight—and not a rancid-tasting potion that cost a crystal fortune. But maybe it was best it hadn't worked. Maybe Earth was too dangerous, as Waverly and everybody else believed.

I closed my eyes, waiting for sleep, thankful that Madame Pearl was an impostor after all, and wondered how I was going to tell my mother I'd lost great-grandfather's silver necklace.

Spencer

At 7:30 A.M. I stood by the south goalpost. This was one event I didn't want to be late for. Not that my life was any big deal. Since my mom left my father and me when I was a kid, our house ceased being a home. I found peace only when riding the waves. I changed my hair color with my changing moods—to lift me out of a funk or cover up the fact I was in one.

But today I sported blue spikes for a different reason, this time in celebration—in honor of the sea where we met. Because this morning was different. I awoke with a swelling of my being, that went beyond my usual swellings! It was a swelling of emotion, a connection to life I'd never felt before. I noticed the magnificence of the clouds as they rolled in from the ocean, the chirping of seagulls, the smell of the sea air. I felt a joy that went way beyond a hundred-thousand score on a Surf Slam 3000 video game, a DVD copy of *Star Wars*, or a year's subscription to *Wipeout*.

But most of all, I felt a connection to her, even though I didn't know her name, and had never heard her voice. Was I obsessed or possessed? If Chainsaw caught wind of my innermost thoughts and feelings, he'd punch me out for sure. I wanted to give her flowers, buy her candy, serenade her underneath a balcony, write her poetry, carve her initials in a tree. It isn't every day that someone breathes life into you. And her breath seemed purer than any I'd ever known.

Eight-fifteen. I mashed my sweaty palms against my jeans. Eight thirty-two. I unraveled a stick of Wrigley's. Eight forty-five. I kicked an empty Coke can. Nine o'clock. I leaned pessimistically against the goalpost.

The bell rang, beckoning me to arrive on time for U.S. history. I slung my backpack over my shoulder and looked at the desolate field. Maybe my personal lifeguard was a late sleeper. Maybe my ad should have read 3:30 P.M. Maybe I was just a complete idiot.

I waited until nine-fifteen, then I waited until nine-thirty. Gym class began running its way around the track. I sauntered up to the fifty-yard line and, dejected, made my way inside the building, late for first bell.

Lilly

I woke up on the shore, lying on my back facing the burning sun. I had to squint, the sun was so bright. I could tell by its position it was just after nine-thirty. Why wasn't I in the water? Why wasn't I in bed? Where was Bubbles? I felt parched to the bone, extremely thirsty. My palms were wet with water that seemed to come from my own hands. My hair was sticky with sand. I could smell the fishy sea air, and hear the sound of seagulls. I panicked. I couldn't breathe. I must get back to the ocean! I felt like I was moving in slow motion, as if I were in a dream—this must just be a dream.

And then I remembered Madame Pearl. I sat up and got the shock of my life, for dangling from the

bottom of my hips were legs! My fin was gone. Gone! What had I done?

"Madame Pearl!" I screamed in an Earthee voice. "Madame!"

I wigged out—wildly wiggling two skinny legs and ten tiny toes! I'd sold my crystal sea horse collection for these legs, but the reality was terrifying. I was cold, naked, and alone. Why hadn't Madame Pearl told me I'd need Earthee clothes? Suddenly the sun seemed to pulsate, the sky started to spin back and forth and day turned to night.

"This isn't a nude beach!" a woman's voice called.

"Madame Pearl?" I whispered, opening my eyes and gasping in crisp air.

"Put your clothes on!" yelled a wrinkled Earthlady wearing a bright purple hat.

Flustered and confused, I spied a yellow beach towel lying a few inches from me. I grabbed it, and wrapped it around my body. Not satisfied, Earthlady pointed to a pile of clothes lying next to a backpack.

"Get dressed, young lady!"

"But this isn't—" I began.

"You're lucky I found you and not the police!"

The police? I had no choice. I couldn't spend my first day on Earth in jail. I picked up a pink top and a pair of matching shorts. I had seen Earthees before, of course, and I knew how they dressed, but

Earthlady's critical stare made me so nervous I couldn't think straight. The next thing I knew I was putting my arms through the shorts. Flustered, I untangled myself and tried to put them on where they belonged. But in my panic, I shoved both legs into one leg hole. I stumbled, fumbled, and tumbled around on the sand.

Finally I stuck my new two legs into different holes and struggled to pull the shorts up. I tried to fasten the button but the shorts were too tight. So I let it go and reached for the shirt.

I tried inserting my head. Choking, I realized I had an arm hole. I rearranged the top and managed to pull it down, but it was much too big and hung off my shoulders like seaweed clinging to the edge of a rock. The shirt came down to my knees, so I tied it around my waist.

I knew I must have been completely dressed when Earthlady grinned with relief.

"You kids are always breaking the rules!" she chided, like a grandma.

An Earthee! Speaking to me, as if I were one of her own kind. Fascinated, I forgot my fear. In any case, she seemed as harmless as a starfish. I stared at her crinkly beige skin and her purple straw hat, her fiery attitude hunching her over more than her aging years.

"You're too pale to lay out without clothes," she

scolded, but in a softer voice. "And you should wear a hat like mine. The sun'll ruin that color job!"

I nodded respectfully, and shoved white open-toed shoes on my two new feet. My two new feet! I was a real Earthee!

Earthlady continued to observe me. I tried to stand up, but I immediately fell over.

"I just bought these legs," I joked, choking the words out.

"You must have gotten up too quickly," she said, extending her hand.

"Blood rushed to my head."

She guided me straight up and held me steady as we began to walk—I for the first time in my life!

"You forgot your backpack," Earthlady said.

"But that's not—" I began, but she had already left me to kindly retrieve the bag.

I teetered on one leg, then the other. I clung to the lifeguard stand. I didn't have water for support, and the air was so thin. Okay, Lills, I said to myself. Either walk to Seaside High or swim all the way to the freezing Atlantic!

"You're dehydrated!" the woman said, pulling a bottle of water from her huge canvas purse.

I pressed my lips around the opening and sucked the contents down in one gulp.

"Oh, my. You are thirsty!"

She helped steady me. I coughed on the smoke from her cigarette. It was hard enough breathing pure air without having to breathe smoke.

"Which way to Seaside High?" I asked, choking, as she helped me put on the backpack.

She pointed past the beach to the hill, where a large school overlooked the Pacific Ocean.

"Well, in that case, you're late, kid," she said sternly. "You'd better get moving!"

"I'm walking as fast as I can," I said, starting to balance on my own.

I stepped on shells, cigarette butts, and empty soda cans. But I quickly recovered and marched up to the top of the beach, where I walked on deep, green grass. It bent easily and felt cushiony, even tickling my toes. A paved hilly road lined with palm trees led to Seaside High School. I was exhausted when I arrived at the entrance. An actual Earthee school! It was much bigger than Pacific Reefs High.

I was breathing and walking pretty well by now. I once read it takes a whole year for an Earth child to stand, much less walk, and I'd done it in less than an hour! Maybe mermaids are a higher life form after all.

Earthdudes and dudettes were leaning against palm trees, walking briskly up stairs, and sitting on the lawn. Tall ones, short ones, skinny and fat, red-

haired and yellow-haired. Girls, boys, and some kids whose gender I couldn't tell.

Would they know I was a mermaid? Would they pounce on me? Harpoon me? I sucked in a deep breath of air and slowly walked up the front stairs, with the help of the railing, but a girl making out with her boyfriend blocked the way. I carefully stepped around them and opened a huge wooden door. I entered a corridor filled with tall cabinets, smooth to my touch, not rusted like the metal at home. One minute it smelled like water lilies, then the next it smelled like an old finball. I read the signs hanging on the walls: MATH CLUB MEETING CANCELED. CONGRATULATIONS, SHARKS, ON A WINNING YEAR! FESTIVAL OF FIREWORKS—FRIDAY NIGHT.

I was mesmerized by all the Earthly activity—laughing, shouting, running, kissing. Some Earthteens dressed as if they'd come straight from the Underworld—tattoos, pierced ears, noses, eyebrows, and tongues. Others dressed as if they'd come from a finball game. Many looked at me as I walked by. Could they tell I was a mermaid? I felt dizzy and leaned against a cabinet to catch my breath.

A guy in a GO SHARKS! shirt approached me, leaned in, and reached his hand to my side. I jumped away.

"That's my locker, chick."

Shocked, I raced away and was thrust into the

middle of a crowd of briskly walking teens. I scanned their faces but none was my Earthdude.

I noticed a wall clock. Nine fifty-five. I was way late for our stadium meeting. And where was the stadium, anyway? Where was he? I peered into a laboratory classroom. Then I looked into an office where a flustered woman was sorting papers at a cluttered wooden desk. Apparently I looked lost.

"May I help you?" the round Earthwoman asked. She seemed to be helpful and trusting.

"I'm looking for—"

"You must be Candy Hartman!" she exclaimed. "I'm Mrs. Linwood, the school secretary. We've been expecting you! I have all your paperwork here." She reached among the papers scattered on her desk. "Welcome to Seaside!"

"But I'm not—"

"Prepared? I know. It's hard joining school at the end of the year. But with your father being with the government, I'm sure you're used to it! Quite exciting, really. But mum's the word!" she said, strangely motioning her hand over her lips.

"We've assigned you to Mr. Costello's class. I'll show you the way," she said, taking me by the arm. "You'll fit right in!"

Fit right in? But I just learned to walk an hour ago!

I was supposed to be in predators and prey class

right now. My out-of-water tardiness was turning into a full-day's absence.

My cherub-faced escort stopped at a crowded classroom. Is this where Earthdude studied? A thousand wide-eyed sharks were staring at me! All I wanted to do was get my locket and leave. But suddenly I not only had legs, but new clothes, and now a new name.

"Good morning, Ms. Hartman, take a seat, please," the teacher said to me. He looked like Mr. Dorsal in cheap pants.

The room was fascinating. Everyone sat on wooden seats with small tables attached, in neat rows. Lights hung from the ceiling, and the walls were plastered with pictures and maps.

I folded my new legs together under my chair and quickly became stuck. Students stared at me as my legs banged against the desk. I noticed their legs dangled, their feet touching the floor.

"This isn't yoga class!" said the leering girl who sat next to me.

The clock read ten-thirty! I was stuck here, trapped from moving forward on my mission. But suddenly my new surroundings engaged me, tantalized me with the reality of all I'd ever dreamed of. I, Waterlilly, was suddenly an Earthdudette myself! I immediately became engrossed with my Earth-school environment.

I finally untangled my legs and peered around the room, making mental notes. A map of Earth, pictures of a pasty man with fluffy white-coral hair, and a thin man with a huge black hat and beard. Another darker man with a mustache and the words, "I have a dream." If Mrs. Current could see me now!

I had learned a lot in Earth history, but a lifetime of study couldn't have prepared me for a real Earthee class. And the Earthees themselves were interesting—blonde girls with blue makeup on their eyelids, shorts, short skirts, dresses, chunky canvas shoes with string ties, or open-toed shoes. And each girl had different colored toenails—pink, purple, green. I wondered if it was cosmetic paint or if they were born that way.

I glanced out the window, which gave a thrilling view of the sea in the distance. I watched the waves crashing against the shore. It was an incredible perspective, breathtakingly beautiful. I'd never seen the ocean from such a height.

"Candy . . . Candy?" Mr. Costello shouted, just as Mrs. Current always shouted at me. At least some things on Earth were the same. "Can you name the four men sculpted in rock on Mount Rushmore?"

Rock group? I thought. "Of course!" I answered confidently. "John, Paul, George, and Ringo!"

The class burst into laughter. A cute guy sitting next

to me—who looked like Beach, only instead of white hair, he had sandy blond hair—nudged me in the legs. Everyone stared and giggled. I slunk back, feeling stupid.

"Miss Hartman, this is social studies, not MTV one-oh-one."

The class laughed even more.

"Do you even know where Mount Rushmore is?"

The cute guy leaned toward me. "Tennessee," he whispered.

"Tennessee!" I shouted.

The class laughed even louder.

I stared at him with contempt. "I thought it was," he whispered, shrugging his shoulders.

"Settle down, class," Mr. Costello said. "Now let's review the presidential elections."

I was fascinated with the rest of his lecture and forgot about the necklace and the time. Presidents, the electoral college, voting. I had never been interested in school in my whole life! But I seemed to be the only one listening. One boy had his head resting on his desk. The girl in front of me was scribbling hearts in a pink journal. Another boy was watching moving pictures on a small screen in his lap. In the sea all students were attentive, like merpuppets.

Suddenly the bell rang.

Mr. Tennessee picked up my social studies text

while the other students left the classroom.

"My name's Calvin."

"My name's . . ."

"I know your name. It's cool to meet you, Candy."

"Yeah . . . totally glacial," I said, distracted. "Hey Calvin," I said inching close. "I need help. Can you help me find—"

"Your next class?" he interrupted.

What if Earthdude was sitting in my next class? I held out the slip of paper with my class schedule.

"Cool, you have geography. Same as me! This is your lucky day. I'll show you the way."

"Just hurry," I said.

The moon was ticking.

Spencer

omebody die?" Robin teased, as she and Chainsaw found me spacing out at my open locker—a dumping ground for CDs, video games, candy wrappers, and books I'd never opened.

Robin was a mother's laundry dream. All dark colors. Never an accidental red bleeding into white. No need for bleach, no need for separate washes. I think the only reason Robin had a crush on me was because I changed my hair color with my changing mood. And my colors were all dark as well: black, purple, blue. She thought I was her soulmate. One day, I'll show up with white hair to see how much she really cares.

"Yeah, Droopy, one minute you're skipping like a

schoolgirl in love and the next you look as if your mommy took away your Nintendo," Chainsaw razzed.

"Go away," I said, grabbing my Gameboy from my locker shelf.

"It's that fantasy girl," Robin teased, with more than a hint of jealousy. "I'm sick for one day and some babe steps in and wins your heart. Or should I say swims in?"

"Yeah, ever since yesterday morning he's been on a major mood swing," Chainsaw quipped.

"Was she really pretty?" Robin asked hesitantly, like she was waiting for a bomb to drop.

"She was beautiful!" Chainsaw answered. "And never to be seen again!"

"Too bad." Robin smiled, cozying up to me. "But I'm here, if you need someone to resuscitate you again."

"Maybe she was a swimming instructor," Chainsaw suggested.

"She was alone," I said, shaking my head.

"Maybe she was a lifeguard," Chain said.

"Seaside's lifeguards wear red. She was wearing green," I said, glaring.

"Then maybe she was a mermaid!" he declared loudly.

"What makes you say that?" I exclaimed, dropping

my books on the floor. I hadn't said anything to Chainsaw about my crazy hallucination.

"Makes sense. She's beautiful, swims in the ocean better than you do, saves your life, and disappears in the water."

"Sure, a mermaid," Robin teased dramatically. "And you know what mermaids are like—they demand pearls and lobster, live in underwater castles, have kings for fathers and stare at themselves in their mirrors. You'd better stick with humans, Spence. We're not so vain."

"Enough!" I said.

Chainsaw opened his locker and he and Robin giggled to themselves.

"Maybe I should start wearing green," Robin said.

I slammed more texts into my backpack, wondering if I'd ever see her again, wondering if I'd ever really seen her in the first place.

Lilly

I chewed on my backpack strap, anxiously waiting for Calvin while he gathered notebooks from his locker.

"You've got to help me! I'm looking for this guy," I shouted urgently. "He has my necklace, and I desperately need to get it back!"

"Did he steal it?" he asked angrily.

"Not exactly, but I have to get it back, now!"

"Is he your boyfriend? You didn't tell me—"

"I don't even know his name."

"Then how did he get your necklace?"

Enough with the questions! I didn't have time for this. But instead I was cordial. "I saved him when he was swimming and he accidentally yanked it off."

"So you're a heroine," he said flirtatiously.

"And you can be a hero by finding him," I said, with a wink.

"All right. What does he look like?"

I stared across the hallway and noticed an Earthdude with dark-blue hair picking up textbooks up from the floor and cramming them into his locker. I couldn't see his face, but his build was similar to Earthdude's.

"Kind of like him," I said pointing. "But with dark red hair."

"We'll find him at lunch," Calvin promised, slamming his locker shut.

Spencer

Nothing is as boring as the predictable Mr. Parker's quarterly lecture as he laments the horrors of our class's GPA. We're close to our final exams—two weeks until summer break. But instead of making plans for my freedom, I was daydreaming about my enslavement to a fair maiden's kiss. I wrote her name in my notebook: Cassandra, Margaux, Juliet. And then I gazed out the window and there she was!

I mean really! I wasn't daydreaming—it was her! Walking on the grass, bright as sunshine, twinkling blue eyes, glistening, sparkling smile, her yellow hair dangling against her porcelain skin.

All that separated us was the window, a row of

hedges, and Seaside's answer to Troy Aikman—Calvin Todd.

"I have to go to the bathroom," I shouted, gathering my books and standing up, without ever taking my eyes off her.

"Excuse me, Spencer?"

"I have to go!"

The class roared with laughter.

"Seems you'll be doing more reading in the can than in my class," Mr. Parker said, referring to the stack of books in my hand.

"Oh . . . yeah." I stammered awkwardly, and slammed the books on his desk as I ducked out of class.

My heart pulsed out of my chest. I felt the adrenaline surge through my body just like when I drive the 3-D mega-speedboat racer at the Seaside Arcade. And just like my boat in hyper-overdrive, I slammed into walls and other obstacles.

"Hey! Watch out, jerk!" one student yelled.

What was I going to say when I found her? Would I thank her or just stare into her ocean blue eyes? Or would I mumble nonsense? Or groan in pain after Calvin Todd obliterated me for stepping on his turf?

Thump thump thump! My engine was throbbing overtime as I threw open the front doors, sped down the front stairs, and raced across the lawn.

She wasn't there! I couldn't swallow, my heart was pulsing up through my throat. Had it been a mirage? But why would I hallucinate Calvin Todd?

I ran back into the building and started searching the first floor. I passed the senior classes, since she didn't seem old enough. But why would she be with Calvin? If she were his girlfriend I would have seen her before. Was she a transfer?

I stepped into Mr. Green's English class.

"Yes. Can I help you?" the weaselly-looking teacher inquired.

"Uh . . . ," I said, glancing at the students whose heads were buried in texts.

"Yes?"

"I . . . uh . . . need chalk." I stammered, stalling to get a better look at the students. I didn't see her or Calvin Todd.

"Chalk?"

"Yes, chalk!"

"You don't have to shout at me," the Weaselman said, suddenly unweasellike.

"Uh, sorry, man."

"Do you need one piece or a whole pack?"

"One piece," I answered quickly, waiting for a blonde girl in the third row to lift up her head. But it was just head cheerleader Linda Wilson.

I inched my way into the aisles and craned my neck

to see the girls in the last row.

"Here," the Weaselman said, offering a piece to me, but suddenly pulling back.

"Is this for a teacher . . . or for graffiti?"

"No one uses chalk for graffiti, Mr. Green. They use spray paint."

"Quite right. Do you need an eraser?"

"No, thanks!" And I dashed out of class.

I gasped for breath as I climbed the stairs to the second floor and pressed my face into Franklin's English lit class. No Calvin Todd, no Cassandra.

I headed straight for Johnson's bio lab. I flew up and down the lab aisles while students prepared to dissect frogs.

"Move!" Sherri Leonard commanded as I backed into her. "You aren't even in this class."

"Yes, Spencer, what are you doing here?" Mr. Johnson inquired. "You have bio on Mondays, Wednesdays, and Fridays. Need more chalk?" he asked, referring to the single piece I was still holding.

"I . . . uh . . . seemed to have lost my safety goggles—"

"I didn't see an extra pair this morning," Mr. Johnson said, trying to remember. "But let's take a look."

He was truly searching for them!

I tapped my fingers nervously against my jeans, the

chalk streaking my leg, while the entire class checked underneath desks and tables, and around beakers.

"That's okay, Mr. Johnson. I'll just use my ski goggles," I said, inching toward the door.

"Here they are!" Kim Ling called, swinging a pair of goggles from her fingers.

I quickly grabbed them, muttered thanks, and ducked into the hallway.

"Those were mine!" I heard a guy call out.

The hallways were empty, except for me running frantically through the school with goggles and chalk.

I peeked my head in Michaels' U. S. history class. "Is Calvin Todd in this class?" I asked. "I have an urgent message for him."

"No," Mr. Michaels replied. "He has this class first bell."

I peeked my head into the music room. Students were dressed in white-and-blue uniforms for band rehearsal, tuning squeaky tubas and trombones.

I was running out of classrooms to check. Soon the principal would notice the lone student sprinting through the corridors, stealing school supplies! I bumped into Mr. Caldwell, a wiry school security guard whose fiery glance could give you sunburn.

"No running in the halls," he said, grabbing my shoulder.

"I'll have to remember that," I responded breathlessly.

"Where's your hall pass?"

"My hall pass? I'm on an errand," I said, wiping the chalk streaks off my jeans.

"A hall pass is mandatory, even for errands."

I glanced past Mr. Caldwell into Hanover's geography class and glimpsed Calvin Todd sitting in the front row.

"What class do you have now?" Caldwell demanded.

"Uh? Class? This one."

"Next time I'll need to see a hall pass or you'll receive a detention," he warned, opening Mrs. Hanover's geography class door for me. I boldly stepped inside. The teacher was using her pointer to highlight Germany.

Calvin Todd stared at me from the front row. And in the back row sat my dream girl!

She was a glistening angel girl. The air around her sparkled. My glistening angel girl chewing anxiously on her pencil, staring at the clock above the window, looking frightened and agitated, as if she were late for an appointment.

I stood frozen as the door closed behind me. I gazed straight at her, but I felt the other students eye-balling me. And especially Mrs. Hanover.

"May I help you, Mr. Stone?"

That caught the attention of Angel Girl. Her blue

eyes stared up at me with delight just as they had in the ocean.

"May I help you?" Mrs. Hanover bellowed again.

The class waited for my answer.

"Mr. Stone!" she said, tapping her pointer against the chalk board, breaking my spellbound gaze. My own chalk was melting in my sweating hand.

"Uh . . ." I stammered, glancing around for help. My angel girl had saved my life in the water, but in Mrs. Hanover's bone dry classroom I was on my own. "I need a map," I said, noticing all the maps on the wall.

"A map?"

"Yes . . . uh . . . for English class."

"A map for English class? Whose English class?"

"Uh . . . Mrs. Brockman's."

"Why do you need a map for English class? What are you studying?"

My mind was a blank. I desperately scoured the room with my eyes for inspiration. I spied a copy of *Hamlet* poking out of a student's book bag.

"Shakespeare."

"The author? Or one of his plays?"

I glanced back at my dream girl, who was staring back at me with the same glow that had warmed the cold Pacific.

"Mr. Stone!"

"Uh . . . *Hamlet*. We need a map of London."

"But *Hamlet* takes place in Denmark!"

The class laughed at my stupidity. I scratched my head like an idiot. "Oh, yeah," I mumbled. "That's why we need the map—no one in class knew where Denmark was, since they don't play in the NFL," I joked.

Everyone laughed, even dream girl. "One kid even thought it bordered Germany!" I announced, hamming it up.

"It does, Mr. Stone!" Mrs. Hanover corrected, using her pointer to highlight Denmark and Germany.

"Oh," I said, no longer the comedian but the fool.

The class giggled again, at my expense. Mrs. Hanover fumbled through her metal cabinet and pulled out a weathered world map.

"Now this is England, where Shakespeare lived," she said condescendingly. "And over here is Denmark, where Hamlet lived. And this, Spencer, is America, where you live, and are standing like an idiot in front of my class making a complete fool of yourself."

Most kids are afraid of bullies. The biggest bully in our school was Mrs. Hanover.

I was surprised she didn't hit me over the head with the map. I could see from her glaring eyes she was thinking about it. The giggles continued as she handed me the rolled-up map. I could no longer bear to look at my angel girl.

In my fantasies of our reunion, I had imagined her running toward me on the beach as I waxed my surfboard, embracing me with passion—not watching me drown again, this time in a sea of geography. She had seen me get hit in the head by my own surfboard and get hit over the head by Mrs. Hanover's sarcasm. She must have thought I was the biggest dork in the world. After trying so hard to find her, I suddenly wanted to be anywhere else but in front of her eyes. She should have let me sink to the ocean floor.

Lilly

I jumped up from my seat. I was really getting used to these legs. But Mrs. Hanover got to the door first, her pointer extended—blocking my way.

"I'm in the middle of my lesson," Mrs. Hanover growled. "Where do you think you're going?"

"It's an emergency!" I said.

I hadn't recognized Earthdude when he'd first entered class, with his dark-blue hair, black *Abbey Road* T-shirt (just like my CD!) and torn jeans, instead of dark-red hair and a wet suit. But when I saw those velvet lips, that chiseled jaw, I knew I had my Earthee! He was quirky and totally lunar, changing his hair color with the changing tide. I laughed when he didn't

seem to know anything about Earth at all. And then he was gone.

"Find your seat!" Mrs. Hanover commanded. "You're disrupting my class."

Mrs. Hanover walked back toward her desk, but I didn't move and she bumped into me. Her pointer dropped to the floor.

"Child!" she said with an evil glare, bending her titanic body over, leaving a clear path to the door.

I raced out of the classroom and into a hallway filled with glittery white-and-blue students wearing huge feathery hats and carrying musical instruments that sounded like bellows from a whale. I pushed my way through. Which way had Earthdude gone? Left? Right?

I chose left and raced down the stairwell, where a teacher was holding the door open for her musical students. "Did you see a guy in a black shirt with blue hair?" I asked desperately.

"The guy kicking the lockers from one end of the hall to the other?"

I nodded my head with a cheeky smile.

"I told him to get a drum," she said, pointing toward the exit.

Spencer

Where were the senior bullies when I really needed one? To shove me into a locker and put me out of my misery! I'd blown everything. In one period my humiliation would have spread like a computer virus! Chainsaw and Robin would have ten minutes of new jokes on me. But really, what did that matter? Only *her* opinion mattered. And she had seen everything through those angel blue eyes.

I had to get away. The beach was my only solace, my surfboard my only friend.

Lilly

Why did Earthdude run off? Maybe he didn't recognize me. Did I blend in that well with the other Earthees? Maybe Madame Pearl's potion had worked too well.

I ran to the back of Seaside High, where I finally found the stadium. Thirty Earthteens sprinted around the track. Everyone was wearing white shirts and blue shorts. And not one of them sported blue hair.

I saw a group of students sitting on the steps.

Exhausted, I tried to catch my breath. A girl sitting on the first step was engrossed in a book.

"Did you see a guy with blue hair?" I asked her.

She shook her head, not taking her eyes off the book. Seaside's white-and-blue band could have noisily

paraded right by her and she wouldn't have looked up.

"What time is it?" I asked.

She held the book with one arm and extended her other, exposing her watch. Eleven forty-five.

I couldn't see the ocean from here, but I could feel it calling me. I had been so close to completing my mission, and now success seemed so far away. I couldn't spend any more time scouring the Earth. My necklace and my Earthdude had disappeared.

I only had one choice. I had to go home! Tell Waverly all my new experiences—Earthdudes in blue jeans, Earthdudettes with different-colored toenails, and me walking through a crowded corridor instead of swimming through a winding tunnel. But worse, I'd have to confess to the crime of borrowing and losing a family heirloom. Take all that was due me, and remember my Earthly experience with melancholy, far underneath the waves in a frigid boarding school in the Atlantic.

I could feel the ocean's waves inside me. I took off my shoes and walked down Seaside High's warm paved road, wanting to feel all there was to feel through my Earthly feet for the last time. I found the warm, grainy sand comforting, yet sad. I was leaving my dreams behind, as I made my way down the sandy beachfront. I passed the lifeguard stand and raced along the tide, not letting it catch my feet. Out of

breath, I climbed up on the rocks underneath the pier, my sandals swinging from my fingers. I leaned over the water's edge, imagining what it would be like to have the water tickle my toes.

I wondered if I would now be a famous merexplorer, celebrated throughout Pacific Reef's history as the one who made it back, winning awards, featured on talk shows, pictured in encyclopedias—but knowing in reality that I'd only be able to tell Waverly of my experience. I stood up and, for one final time, gazed back at my new world and all its beauty—Seaside High peering over the hill, palm trees extending their branches to the sky, happy tourists sunning underneath the glistening sun.

And outside Mickey's Surfboard Hut—one Earthdude with illuminating blue hair!

It couldn't be.

I raced back over the rocks, jumped onto the warm sand, and ran as hard as I could.

"It's me!" I proclaimed, waving my arms. "It's me!"

Out of breath, I finally reached my Earthdude, who stared wide-eyed, like he was drowning again.

Spencer

I didn't recognize her sweet voice at first. I'd only seen her—glistening underwater, sparkling through an algebra classroom window, and giggling in Hanover's class. Now she was standing in front of me almost out of breath herself.

What could I say to her now that I had the chance? I had waited what seemed like an eternity to see her again. Hadn't I made a fool of myself enough today?

Still, I was elated. While she recovered her breath and pushed back her hair, I wished it were my hand exposing her perfect face. A million questions raced through my mind. Had she seen my ad? Where was she from? What was she doing in the ocean yesterday? I could barely believe that this beauty had pressed her savory lips on mine! But the words turned to alphabet soup when I opened my mouth.

"You know who I am, don't you?" she asked forcefully.

I now realized why she was here. Not to let me thank her, like I'd originally intended, but just to get her necklace back.

I nervously fingered the chain in my pocket, as if I had ripped it off from a jewelry store. "I waited at the stadium. Did you get my note?"

"Yes, but I overslept. I looked all over school for you," she said, agitated. "But I thought your hair was dark red."

"I change it every week."

"Is that normal? Do you change your name every week, too?"

"It's normal for me. But my name's always Spencer."

"Well, Spencer, can I have the necklace?" she asked suddenly.

If I returned it to her now, I'd lose her. She'd show up for school tomorrow, hand in hand with Calvin Todd. I'd be destined for the rest of my high-school days to watch her sparkling smile radiate toward him at football games as he scored touchdowns and more. I only had one choice. "You saved my life, and I don't even know your name," I said urgently.

85

"Well . . . people around here call me Candy."

"Candy, I wanted to ask you something first. Before I give you back the necklace," I began, my grip slipping on the surfboard as I tried to muster up courage. "I'd like to pay you—"

"I don't want money," she insisted. "I want my necklace."

"But I want to thank you, properly. After school . . . Take you to the pier for dinner . . . Then I'll give it back."

She didn't respond, but impatiently looked toward the ocean.

"What's your favorite restaurant?"

"I can't stay for dinner," she blurted out.

I glanced around, wishing Chainsaw were here. What would he say now? Then I noticed the Starbucks on the pier. "Then how about a cup a coffee now, on the pier?"

She looked up with sudden interest. "I've never been on the pier before."

"There's a first time for everything," I said, leading her to my favorite hangout.

Lilly

I had a few hours left before my potion lost its effect, but for safe measure my plan was this: spend a little time with Earthdude—I mean Spencer—make him feel he's not indebted to me anymore, and at the same time catch a few more Earthly sights, smells, and tastes. After half an hour, I'll say, "It's been great, thanks, gotta go." He'll hand over great-grandpa's necklace, and when he looks away for a second, I'll dive safely back into the water.

I was overwhelmed by the pier's magical brilliance. Previously I had only glimpsed it from the rocks below or viewed it from the ocean, miles away. And now it was within my reach. A huge white wheel with red and silver dangling chairs stood in the distance,

nautical shops lined the boardwalk, and tiny huts sold T-shirts, sunglasses, and shell necklaces.

I wheezed from climbing the stairs and leaned on the boardwalk railing that overlooked the ocean, trying to recover my breath.

"What kind of coffee do you like?" Spencer asked kindly, leading me into a shop with a freakish mermaid on the sign.

Latte, Frappuccino, cappuccino. The funny words I read meant nothing to me. I didn't even know what coffee was! "I'll have whatever you have," I said.

"Two double lattes," he ordered.

I'd never thought I'd even visit Earth for a minute, much less a day, and here I was standing in a shop ordering drinks!

I ran my fingers over everything—drinking cups, bottles, hardened treats inside beautiful papers. I gazed at objects shaped like sponges and sea cucumbers beneath a glass counter.

"Want something?" he offered, close behind me.

"Do you?" I asked, looking for guidance.

"Sure. But you pick this time. Anything in the store," he said proudly.

I was overwhelmed with choices and scanned the counter. There were mudlike squares displayed on a dish, a jar filled with red and white striped tubes.

Overwhelmed, I pointed to a solid white cup with a black label.

"I'd love some tips!" I exclaimed.

"You're hilarious!" he said, as he and the perky counter girl laughed at my choice.

"Two scones, please," he ordered, pointing to a puffy sand-colored orb inside the case.

He led me outside where we sat on a wide wooden bench facing the ocean. I ingested my Earthly world at the same time I ingested my hardened spongy scone. Children ran along the beach, a young couple splashed each other in the water, two elderly Earthees walked arm in arm, an athletic man ran along the shoreline with his panting black dog.

"So tell me everything," Spencer began between bites. "Were you swimming or surfing the other day? Where did you live? Why did you transfer? Where do you live now?"

"Uh . . . I live west."

"By the planetarium?"

"Closer to the beach . . ."

"Oh . . . by Yates Bluff."

"What about you?" I asked, as a seagull called out overhead.

"I live with my dad in Pacific Cliffs."

"What about your mother?"

89

"My mom left us when I was a kid."

"Do you ever see her?"

"No. In fact, I never even got to say good-bye to her."

"You never got to say good-bye?"

"She ran off with a used car salesman. My dad wanted her to trade in our Chevy and she traded him instead. Now we only buy new cars!" he said, laughing.

"But that's so sad. Where I'm from nobody ever leaves anyone—"

"I pretty much raised myself with the help of my friend Chainsaw, my surfboard, and a Blockbuster card."

"A Blockbuster card?" I asked.

"What's your story, Candy?"

"Uh . . . me? I like to swim, my parents get majorly on my nerves, I hate high school. And I have a best friend, Waverly. But my life is so boring! It's not worth asking about. Can't we just sit?" I asked. "It's been a long day."

"Oh, sure," he said, leaning back and staring off toward the ocean.

"Besides, I'd rather know about you. Do you hang here often?"

"Not during school. But don't worry. Seaside's a tourist trap, so no one really can tell who's who if you skip out of class. A major mistake, if you ask me, to

90

have a school so close to a beach."

I stared up at his chiseled face, the light in his eyes. I'd been so distracted with these spectacular Earthly sights, that I failed to notice the spectacular sight right in front of me.

Spencer caught my gaze and, embarrassed, I turned away. "Well, Spencer . . . it's been . . ."

"Don't you like your coffee?" he asked, breaking the white plastic rim of his own cup into tiny pieces.

"Uh, sure," I said. I took a gulp and almost choked.

"Are you okay?"

"It tastes like mud!"

His eyes sparkled when he laughed, as if I had said the cutest thing he'd ever heard.

"I'll get you some water," he offered with a smile. "You sit tight."

"That's okay. I have to—" I began. But he bolted off.

I leaned back on the bench and pulled my legs up and hugged them with all my might. Spencer was really special. I felt drawn to him the same way I felt drawn to the ocean. I wondered what it would be like to sit in class with him every day, have him teach me to surf, lie in the grass and look up at the puffy clouds. But he'd be returning with my water and I'd have to get my necklace and leave.

I felt a tap on my shoulder.

"Yeah, Spencer?" I said, turning around.

"Can you spare some change?" a scruffy man asked.

I felt frightened. Where was Spencer? Would the man hurt me since I didn't have any coins? Did he have a knife? I felt like I was in the Underworld again without shark mace.

"I'm sorry, I don't have any money with me," I confessed. "But you're welcome to this," I said, handing him my coffee.

"Hey, Candy," Spencer called, anxiously running back.

"Thank you, miss," the man said, his withered face lighting up like the sun. He took the coffee as Spencer approached. "Most people don't even make eye contact!" said the man as he turned to leave.

The man turned his attention to Spencer.

"She has a pretty smile and a gracious heart. Don't let her get away," he said, and sauntered off.

"Speaking of leaving," I began, rising. "It's been totally—"

"But I don't know anything about you," he said, handing me the plastic bottle. "Here, everyone likes water."

"I can't live without it!" I said, laughing at my inside joke. He smiled fondly. I twisted off the cap, like I'd seen an Earthlady do earlier, and I sucked it down in one gulp.

Spencer gave me the same look that Earthlady had. "Man, you must be thirsty!"

I smiled and shrugged my shoulders. He leaned his arm against the railing, blocking my escape. I glanced down at his *Abbey Road* T-shirt.

"I have that compact disc at home," I said.

His eyes widened. "No way. You like the Beatles? So many girls at school are only wiggy about current bands. But the Beatles were real musicians!"

"The Beatles, the ocean, saving you. You might say we're connected," I said.

His face flushed and he immediately took a sip of his latte. A freakish mermaid on the side of the cup stared me in the face.

"Mermaids don't have two tails!" I said, looking at the drawing. "And crowns are so five cycles ago!" I rolled my eyes.

"You're funny," he said, with a laugh. "You know what? My best friend thinks you're a mermaid!"

I gasped. Was my identity obvious? Had he known all along? But Spencer's grin reassured me that he was only joking.

"Do you believe in mermaids?" I asked playfully, but secretly hoping for a positive response.

"Like I believe in trolls and gnomes!" he exclaimed.

We both laughed. He had the cutest smile, the corners of his mouth turned up sweetly. I wondered what

it would be like to kiss his lips out of the water, to touch his face, his wild blue hair. But he averted his eyes toward the sea.

"Well . . . I better—" I said.

"It's funny," he began, "but when I saw you underwater I thought—"

"That I was a troll?"

"It must have been the lack of oxygen," he said, with reservation. "But I thought I saw a ta—"

"Really, I should be—"

"Why were you swimming so early, anyway?" he asked.

"I love swimming," I defended. "I prefer it to walking."

"Yeah." He smiled. "Me, too!"

He stared at me, his eyes mixed with passion and nervousness.

"Why did you transfer to Seaside?" he asked, looking at a ship on the horizon.

"It was either that or the Atlantic," I replied truthfully enough, placing my foot on the railing so that it was almost touching his.

Spencer was so different. And not just because he was an Earthee. He was different from every soul I had ever encountered. I felt a connection without our sharing words, a connection just sharing space.

94

"So, is Calvin your boyfriend?" he asked in a halting voice.

"Are you kidding? He's so like the dudes back home. He was just trying to help me find you."

"Well . . . then I should thank him," he said sweetly. He looked to the ocean.

I felt a strange pulse deep inside my veins. I could tell by the sun that it was after one o'clock. The moon was on the rise. "I wish I could stay longer," I said, trying to push past him.

But he didn't budge and instead grabbed my hand and led me into Seaside Arcade—a room filled with metal machines, flashing lights, and loud, wild sounds. "This is my favorite place in the world, besides the beach."

I covered my ears.

He stuck four coins into a model of a motorboat and told me to sit inside and steer the wheel. He then got into the next boat.

"Ready?"

"Of course!" I said, having no idea what I was in for. I looked at the screen, but my boat wasn't going anywhere. Then I noticed Spencer was pressing a pedal on the floor, so I copied his moves. My boat began to move. It was wild pretending to be on top of the water, instead of deep below the surface. But I soon

crashed into another boat whose driver flew over-
board.

"Oh, no!" I screamed. "What do I do now?"

"Drive on!" he said, shifting his stick.

"But the man's drowning!"

"You can't save everyone," Spencer teased, swerv-
ing to avoid a lighthouse.

Game Over lit up on my screen. My boat no longer
moved. While Spencer continued to drive his own
boat, I decided to explore the rest of the arcade.

I had heard of guns. I'd even seen some rusted can-
nons at our Pacific Museum. But these two were
pointing at a screen of ghosts.

"Wanna play?" Spencer asked, catching up to me.

I nodded, curious.

Ghosts floated in front of us, like delirious
mermen. We had to shoot them. My stomach turned
over as red blood squirted out from their gun wounds
and their heads popped off. By mistake I shot a girl
with yellow hair. "You play," I said, and handed
Spencer the gun.

"I'm sorry," he said, following me through the maze
of games. "I wanted to show you a good time, but
we're just doing things I want to do."

I stood mesmerized in front of brightly colored
fuzzy animals in a glass case. I tapped the glass, but
the animals didn't move. It took me a moment to

realize they weren't real.

"Which one do you like?"

I pointed to a wide-eyed pink swan.

Spencer maneuvered two white controls on the machine, and a metal crablike claw grabbed the pink fluffy swan and dropped it. Spencer picked the toy out of the chute and proudly handed it to me.

"I love it!" I exclaimed, squeezing it to my chest. "It's the softest thing I've ever touched besides—" I began, as our eyes met.

I wanted to say "your lips." He stared at me with soulful eyes. But I felt a sharp pain shooting through my veins.

"Besides?" he asked, grabbing my arm.

"I gotta go!" I exclaimed, turning away from him and walking out of the arcade.

"But it's only one-thirty," he said, following me along the pier. "What about a ride?" he asked, pointing to a huge wheel with swinging chairs that touched the sky. "You can stay another three minutes."

"Well . . ."

I was enjoying Earth. I would have stayed forever if I could. I wanted to touch, see, smell, and hear everything. What was so important at home that it couldn't wait for a three-minute ride? "Okay!"

Spencer ran to get tickets and came back with a huge blue weblike substance on a stick as well.

"Candy for Candy." He laughed, handing me the stick.

We sat close on the ride. I could feel my legs against his blue pants.

I stuck my finger in the soft weblike treat. Sweet grains slithered on my tongue. "This is amazing—what is it?"

"Don't tell me you've never eaten cotton candy!" he said, taking a bite of the blue cloud.

Suddenly we lifted off the ground. I grabbed Spencer's arm for dear life as we swung into the air. I had never seen a view of the world like this before!

"I feel like a bird!" I said, wide-eyed, when we reached the top.

"You've never been on a Ferris wheel?"

"I've never been higher than the rocks at the pier," I confessed in my excitement. "Look, there's Seaside High School! Look at the students! They're so tiny!" I exclaimed, pointing. "They look like sea horses!"

"Everyone else says ants. You're totally clever."

"Yeah . . . ants," I corrected myself.

"You really have a unique view of the world. You say things no one else would ever say. You do things no one else would ever do."

"Like saving you?" I said, looking at him.

His face turned red. Now he was the one who looked down, pointing. "Hey, look at the steroid-

buffed lifeguards! They don't look so big from up here."

"That was incredible!" I said to Spencer as the attendant let us out.

"Thank you . . . for my life . . . for coming here. I hope we can do it again sometime," he said. "Too bad you have to go."

"Yeah. Too bad." I glanced along the boardwalk. "What's a fun house?"

"You've never been to a fun house, either? Man, you've had a deprived childhood!"

We looked at each other.

"Five more minutes?" I asked.

"Not a second longer, I promise!" Spencer said enthusiastically.

He quickly led me into the creaky house. The floors were bumpy, curvy, and shook from side to side.

I grabbed onto the rails with all my might, my stuffed swan dangled from my shaking fingers. Spencer crossed to the other side and laughed at me. I remained motionless, unsure how to proceed. He extended his hand, and led me safely across the shaky boards. I gave him my swan for safekeeping, and he stuck it securely in his back pocket.

In the next room we stood in front of life-size mirrors. But I didn't look like myself. And neither did he.

Something was terribly wrong! We were stretched, tall and skinny. My length had doubled and my waist decreased to the size of a twig. I felt no pain, but the sight frightened me and I screamed.

Spencer laughed again. He was really enjoying himself at my expense. He must have thought I was a complete idiot. I began giggling to cover my embarrassment. In the next mirror my head and body were short and fat. No longer frightened by these weird reflections, I forced another scream, just to make him think my first scream had been faked as well.

The walls of the next room were painted with flowers. I had read a book about Earth flowers and was trying to identify them when the room went black. Ghosts appeared, flying over our heads. A hairless man, covered with blood, extended his arm toward me, only the hand was missing!

"Spencer!" I reached out for him, but he wasn't there. I hurried away from the ghosts and found myself in another hall of reflections. This time I looked normal, but I was everywhere. A thousand frightened Lillys staring helplessly back at me.

But where was he?

"Hello!" I called again. I couldn't see where I'd come from, or the way to the exit. I felt trapped. I began to panic. "Spencer?"

There was no answer.

"Spencer! I'm over here!"

All I saw was myself, growing redder and redder with fright.

"Where are you?" I shouted.

"Candy?" I finally heard him call.

Suddenly I saw a thousand Spencers. I reached for his outstretched hand, but instead I touched glass.

"I'm over here!" I screamed, totally frightened. I felt a sharp pang in my veins. The moon was rising, and I feared I'd be left for the rest of my life to stare at not two legs, but two thousand.

"Find me!" My hands shook uncontrollably. Water mysteriously dripped from my palms, streaking the reflections as I continued to search for Spencer's hand.

I finally felt something grab me and I screamed.

"It's okay, Candy. You should have told me you were claustrophobic," Spencer said, stroking my arm.

I hugged him with all my might, not letting him go. He stroked my hair. My heart pounded. I'm sure he could feel it pulse out of my chest and beat against his own. I almost didn't want to calm down—it felt so good, being so close to him.

"Now you've saved me, too!" I exclaimed, as we exited the fun house, my pink swan now swinging from my fingers. "We're even."

"It's hardly the same thing," he said. "Anyway,

you've been through a lot today. A new town, a new school."

"I had the best day—ever!"

"Seriously? Me, too. Well, the second best, if you're counting yesterday morning," he added sweetly.

I felt another sharp pang. "I gotta go!" I said urgently, clutching my stomach.

"Are you okay?" he asked, concerned.

"It's just a cramp."

"Let me walk you home," he offered, taking my arm and leading me toward the beach.

"You can't—"

"It's no trouble."

"It's a lot of trouble! More than you know."

"I can call a cab."

"I have to go alone."

"I wanted to take you to a fancy dinner—to a restaurant with a view," he blurted out. "I wanted to present you with roses, a white one for the color of your skin, a yellow one for the color of your hair and a pink one for the way you glow when you smile."

Something moved me deep inside, but I wasn't sure if it was the pulse of the moonrise or the pulse of Spencer.

"I know I sound like a geek," he said, nervously running his fingers through his hair. "But I hope tomorrow . . . What am I saying? Tomorrow you'll be with Calvin."

"Calvin who?"

He smiled, but his eyes were sad. "Thanks again for saving my life—" he said. "I just want to ask you— Listen . . . Seaside's Annual Festival of Fireworks is tomorrow right here on the beach. I guarantee you'll like it more than the hall of mirrors."

"I can't," I said hurriedly. The cramps in my side were killing me.

"I shouldn't have asked," he said, looking at his shoes.

"I don't have time to explain. I have to go!"

"It was cool hanging out with you, Candy. Under the water and out," he teased.

"My friends call me Lilly," I blurted out.

"Lilly."

I smiled. My name flowed like a waterfall from his lips. He awkwardly leaned forward and kissed me on the cheek.

I was being pulled in two different directions. My stomach was rumbling from the imminent moonrise. But there was the ache of belonging to Spencer and not wanting to leave. He was totally scorching. Different from Beach, Tide, Calvin, and any Earth- or merdude I'd ever met. I could feel his soul in mine, as if my heart was in my open hands, reaching out to him. I took in his presence, his beauty, his wacky midnight blue hair, his intoxicating scent. I wanted to be

with him forever, to ride the tremendous wheel again, to see the fireworks, to dance beneath the moonlight.

I grabbed his shirt and pulled him into me. His lips melted against mine.

I knew I'd never see Spencer again. I missed him already, as he stood pressed against the other end of my lips, unaware that we could never meet again.

I had come for one heart, but was leaving two behind.

Spencer

She kissed me! I felt higher than the top of the Ferris wheel! Then something dropped behind me, as she ended our embrace. I turned around to see what it was.

It was the swan. It had fallen from her gentle grasp while we were kissing, into a puddle. I wiped the stains from its pink fur. But when I rose to hand it back to her, she was gone.

Where could she have gone so quickly?

My heart sank as I searched the arcade, Starbucks, and the rest of the pier.

Candy—I mean Lilly—had left me again, as if she had mysteriously swum off like the day she had saved my life.

I leaned on the railing for several minutes, the swan dangling from my hand, and stared out at the waves splashing up against the shoreline.

I realized I still had some tokens left. Might as well crash some speedboats while waiting for Chainsaw. I reached into my pocket, but I found an infinitely more valuable token. The necklace! I had forgotten to give it back. But more importantly, and mysteriously, she had forgotten to take it.

I walked into the dark arcade in high spirits. I was still in the game.

Lilly

I'm in love!" I shouted to Waverly. I twirled around in her pastel pink bedroom that evening as we dressed for Beach's party. I told her everything— about waking up naked, about my new clothes, my new legs, my new name. But I told her mostly about the dreamiest dude I'd ever met. "His kiss was way more magical than anything Madame Pearl could have sold me."

I still felt dizzy, from Spencer, and from my transformation back into a mermaid. At first, my tail moved in slow motion, but as I talked to Waverly, I grew stronger.

I had missed school, but that wasn't unusual for me. What was unusual was that instead of hanging

out at my secret cave, I had gone to Earth.

"You can't be in love with an Earthee! It's prohibited," she said. "But at least you got the necklace back!"

"Oh, no!" I gasped. "I forgot! I was having so much fun, the necklace was the last thing on my mind."

"Lilly!" Wave scolded.

"I've never felt so alive! The pier, the wheel, the candy. Spencer."

"Well, if you play your cards right at Beach's party tonight and your mom learns you're dating a primo heartthrob with a trust fund, maybe she'll let you off easier. And you and Beach can live happily ever after."

"Beach? No way! Spencer is way dreamier. He gave me a swan and he invited me to watch fireworks!"

"Fireworks?"

"Yeah, those colored explosions that fill the sky every year."

"The only colors you should be thinking about are the ones on your outfits."

"You have to understand, Wave. The way you feel about Tide is the way I feel about Spencer. I can't help it if he lives on Earth. That's just logistics."

"You just met him, girl."

"But I feel like I've known him all my life. I know now that something in my life was missing. Love."

"That's the potion talking. It's screwed with your head."

"He's interesting, intelligent. He's totally glacial." I let out a sigh of love.

"Forget him!" she said, putting shell clips in my hair.

"Why can't you be on my side? Don't you want me to be happy?"

"Yes, but here. In the Pacific. If word gets out of your antics, you'll be sent to the Atlantic. Then you'll really be far away from Spencer."

The Atlantic? I felt far enough away from Spencer as it was, and we were only separated by a few miles and an Earthly atmosphere. The Atlantic would be like living in the core of the Earth.

"You're right," I said reluctantly.

"Of course, I am. We'll go to Beach's party. You'll become his girlfriend. And you'll stay in the Pacific," she said, brushing my hair. "And now and then we'll hang out on the rocks at the edge of the pier and look up at Seaside High."

My stomach ached as if an octopus were turning around inside it. I knew Wave was right. I must forget Spencer.

Wave and I arrived at Club Atlantis totally decked out—Wave dripping in an opal dress and I in a

skintight lion-fish print top and tail with golden glitter sprinkled in my hair. Club Atlantis was an open-water dance club fashioned after a historical outdoor Earthee Roman city that had succumbed to the water. Arched columns lined the entrance, and Earthees carved out of rock lined the walls.

A neon sign blinked HAPPY 16TH BEACH. Merkids hung out everywhere—on the steps, in the gardens, over the statues—practically the whole school was there. We floated to the amphitheater where the Screaming Eels were playing "Electric Sunset." I found Beach in the first row. He did look scorching—in a hunky sort of way. And he was flexing for everyone. He was showing off his Shark tattoo to two babes when we arrived.

"I didn't see you at school today," he said very sternly.

"I was studying for tonight," I replied. "Here's your present."

"You can put it over there," he said, pointing to a table just below the stage covered with a mound of presents.

I returned from Present Island to find Wave and Tide dancing with Beach. Beach pulled me close, weighing me down as he hung his thick arm on my shoulder.

"It's good to see you two so snuggly!" Wave said.

I glared at her.

Suddenly the Screaming Eels stopped playing and the lead singer announced a special guest.

"Surprise!" a sexy mermaid in heavy blue eye shadow, a very low-cut red-laced top and matching fin tail called, as she floated to center stage. "Who's the birthday boy?"

Beach floated over Present Mountain and swaggered onstage. "Me! It's me!"

"Well happy birthday, baby!" she sang, giving him a huge hug. The Screaming Eels jammed and the mertart danced. His finball mates hooted and hollered, while pristine mergirls giggled out of embarrassment. Wave turned to me with a cheesy smile.

"Why did you bring me here?" I shouted above the music. I swam up the aisle through the gardens and out the front arch.

"Wait!" Waverly called, following me.

"This is what I have to look forward to for the rest of my life? Beach and his finball friends?" I untied Bubbles' leash. "I don't fit in here! I never have, don't you understand?"

"Lilly—"

"I have to get my heart back—and I'm not talking about that stupid necklace this time."

"But you can't! You can't!" I heard her plead as I sped off.

111

✯ ✯ ✯

I woke up early the next morning for the first time in my life. Three cans of shark mace and bundles of clothes filled my backpack. I raced Bubbles straight to the Underworld. If a shark spotted me, I'd have him for breakfast! That's how fueled by passion I was to see Spencer again. And fortunately for the sharks, there were none in sight.

Closed. The stone sign hung heavy on Madame Pearl's shop like an anchor weighing down my dreams. No clarifications. No "on vacation," or "back in five minutes," or "out to lunch." The word was simple but made my life complicated!

"Madame Pearl?" I yelled. "Madame Pearl?"

There was no response.

"Have you seen Madame Pearl?" I asked a beggar outside her window.

"Madame who?"

"Pearl . . ."

"All the madames are down the street," he said. "Can you spare some change?"

"Have you seen Madame Pearl?" I asked a tattoo artist in the next store. He was painting a sea dragon on a merman's back.

"You're too young to come in here," he scolded, waving his tattooing pen at me. But I held my ground.

I was afraid he was going to paint a serpent on me!

"I'm looking for Madame Pearl."

"Next store."

"She's not in. Do you know where she lives?"

"No one knows where she lives."

I let out a sigh of despair.

I hurried back and banged on her door. Maybe she'd slipped in while I was gone. The heavy door slowly opened with the current.

"Madame?" I called, peeking in.

No one answered.

"Madame, it's Lilly from the other day. The girl who wanted legs."

I looked everywhere. I pulled back the curtain on her potion room. If only Madame Pearl was psychic and sensed how much I needed her! But did I really need her? I noticed the stacks of books and shellboxes on the shelves.

Did the potion call for the eye of a shrimp or a frog? The tongue of a lizard or a turtle?

I looked at the stacks of stone-bound books. *Mood Potions. Party Potions. Just Plain Magic.*

I picked up *Just Plain Magic* and scanned the pages.

"SPELLS—Employer, Spouse, Neighbor. ILLU-SIONS—Disappearing, Card tricks, Conning. TRANSFORMATIONS—Transgender, Anti-aging, Earthee."

There it was! It should be as easy as following a

recipe. I've done that before—I make a killer seaweed stew. I lay the heavy page on a stone bench. It read:

EARTHEE

1 eye of shrimp
1 tongue of frog
1-inch leg of octopus, unfrozen, no skin
Dash of seaweed
Pinch of sea salt
Sprinkle of magic

Combine ingredients and shake vigorously.
Drink under a crescent moon.
Return to sea before following moonrise.
400 calories

Could it be that easy? Thank goodness Madame Pearl was well organized. She had labeled all her ingredients. I grabbed and cut, dashed and pinched, combined and shook the contents. But what about the magic? I found an unmarked box of gold dust—surely that must be the sprinkle of magic. I added it to the horrible yet heavenly sweet mixture and sealed it with a cork. My Earthee potion was ready to go. Hey, I was pretty good at this. Maybe I could open my own shop.

"You forgot the magic!" a voice shouted.

Startled, I dropped the bottle, but before I could

reach it, a thick hand grabbed it.

"Madame Pearl!" I said, breathless.

"Didn't you read the sign?" she asked sternly, floating before me, my bottle clutched in her hands.

"I was desperate! I need another bottle."

"The first potion didn't work?" she asked skeptically. "I don't do refunds."

"It worked perfectly! But I need to make one more trip."

"I thought you spent all your savings?"

"Well . . ."

"So were you going to leave me your lunch money?"

"I was going to write an IOU. Please, Madame Pearl!" I pleaded. "I'd explain, but you wouldn't understand—"

"Wouldn't I?" She glared at me hard. "You're in love!"

"I thought you weren't a psychic."

"You don't need to be a psychic to spot love. You have all the signs. Irrational behavior. Defiance. And that special sparkle in your eyes."

"It shows?"

"It's oozing out of your heart. Besides, no one would go back to Earth, with its polluting cars, salty codfish, or those painful high heels—unless they were in love."

"How do you know so much about Earth?" I asked, amazed.

She paused. Then she pushed back a stack of boxes marked EDIBLE HERBS, dug her thick hands into the sandy floor and pulled out a photograph protected by clear plastic. It captured a handsome man in a sailor suit, holding a white flower.

"I spotted him on a ship while I was swimming one day a long time ago," she confessed in a dreamy voice. "We stared at each other for miles—he on the boat, I in the water. He invited me aboard, but of course I couldn't go. But I followed his ship to dock and I met him early the next morning as an Earthee. He was like a Greek god, and in those days I had a slim figure and golden curls. That was so long ago," she said, tugging at her bulging black skirt. "We were passionately in love. We wed within hours. But I stole away in the night. And I never went back."

"Why not?"

"I wasn't brave—I mean—foolish enough."

"But don't you regret it now?"

"I wasn't much older than you," she said, trying to convince me I was being immature.

"Please, Madame Pearl, let me have the second chance you've always wished for! Don't let me make the same mistake!"

"I could lose my shop!"

"I could lose my soulmate!" I exclaimed.

The word touched her heart and she gazed thoughtfully back at the picture. "Sometimes, when I hear a boat go by, I hear his voice call my name."

"Madame Pearl," I said, looking at her shell clock.

"But you won't take any steps with this potion you made," she suddenly declared in her normal, practical voice. "You need magic!"

"But I already put it in."

"You added golden dust. I can see it shimmering. It won't hurt you. It might make you tired. But it won't give you legs."

"Then what do I do?" I asked desperately.

"Hold the bottle to your heart," she said, handing it to me.

I held it fast.

"Now close your eyes and think of him."

"Is that what you did last time? Think of your old love?" I felt a sudden connection with the old woman.

I closed my eyes, and a huge smile came over my face.

"That's enough," she said.

I uncorked the bottle and gulped the potion down before her eyes. This time I didn't even flinch. "How much do I owe you, Madame Pearl?"

"You're not going to come back just to pay me," she said, gazing again at her sailor, so I quietly drifted away.

Spencer

The next day Lilly didn't show up for school. I didn't see her in the halls, sitting on the front lawn, or in her geography class. Chainsaw didn't see her either, and Robin couldn't care less.

"We're not married!" Calvin muttered, after I approached him at his locker. "How should I know where she is? Who are you, anyway?"

I replayed yesterday's events in my mind. Her excitement over the stuffed swan, eating cotton candy as if for the first time. Graciously handing the beggar her coffee. Clinging to me desperately in the hall of mirrors, and then the way she suddenly pulled me into her and kissed me like a girl who's not afraid of anything. I realized I didn't even know her last name, her address. She was even more mysterious in real life than she had been in my imagination.

Chainsaw, Robin, and I went to the nosebleed section of the football bleachers for lunch. Robin sat a few rows down reading *Rolling Stone*, Chainsaw was watching *The Fugitive* on his million-dollar laptop, while I stood in the last row, facing away from the field, looking for Lilly among the throngs of students milling outside. The bleachers were the highest point at school, save for the flagpole. And I thought we'd look pretty silly if Lilly did wander in and spy me clinging to a pole underneath the stars and stripes.

"You did see her yesterday, didn't you?" I asked, frustrated. "I couldn't have dreamed about her twice?"

"Yeah, dude, I saw her!" Chainsaw said. "But I'm not sure that I didn't dream about her last night. That body? Delicious!"

"Don't talk that way about her!" I said, tossing a plastic cup at him.

"Or me either!" Robin said sarcastically. "I hate it when the two of you fawn all over me!"

"Take a Valium, dude! You'll see her again," Chainsaw said, adjusting his headphones.

"Maybe she got mugged. Or kidnapped."

"It would have been on the news," Chainsaw said. "Her parents would have called the school."

"Maybe they have her locked in a cage!" Robin exclaimed.

"A lot of help you are," I shouted back. But then I thought of my angel, helpless, like a caged bird. "Could it be true?"

"You both need to get out more," Robin complained.

"This is making me crazy!" I shouted.

"Chill out! Maybe she's sick," Chainsaw finally said. "Did you ever think of that? She is human after all."

"She did have cramps at the pier," I remembered, sitting down next to him.

"Sure—it's her girlie time! She took the day off to chew on Midol, eat Ben and Jerry's and bawl her eyes out talking on the phone to her best friend."

"You think so?" I asked eagerly.

"I know so! You've seen how psycho my mom gets—one minute she flies off the handle because the toilet seat's up, the next minute she cries at a Hallmark commercial. Believe me, you're better off not seeing her!"

I returned to my lookout post and leaned on the aluminum railing. Maybe Chainsaw was right. But I couldn't wait until tomorrow to find out.

Mrs. Linwood, our airhead school secretary, was

rummaging through her overstuffed file cabinet when I barged into her office.

"Candy—she didn't show up today. Is she sick?"

"Excuse me?" Mrs. Linwood asked, startled.

"Candy. The transfer student."

"Oh, I met her yesterday. Lovely girl," she said, plopping into her chair.

"Is she sick?" I asked.

"No one called in for her today."

"Do you know where she is?"

"If I did, that information would be confidential."

"She's my lab partner in Mr. Johnson's class. We have an assignment due today," I lied.

"But she just transferred yesterday. How could she have an assignment due today?"

"Ask Mr. Johnson. I don't think it's fair. That's why I need your help!"

"But—"

"It's thirty percent of our final grade. I could fail the whole quarter! He's a madman, really."

"Well . . ."

"Please, it's up to you to save the day," I begged.

"All right, all right. Let me take a look at the records." She shuffled through the heap of files on her desk and picked up a Post-it. "One call was made to her house at noon. No one answered. They didn't have a machine, so we couldn't leave a message."

She went back to her bloated file cabinet.

"Can you call again, please? Now? She's also supposed to go to the fireworks with me tonight," I confessed.

"With you?" she asked, skeptically.

"Please?" I begged.

"Oh, all right." Mrs. Linwood pulled my angel's record from her cabinet and punched in the phone number.

It rang forever. Mrs. Linwood shook her head and began to put the phone down. "Hello? Hello?" she suddenly said. "Yes, Seaside High School calling. Candy was supposed to be is school today, but no one has . . . yes . . . Candy Hartman . . . She transferred here yesterday . . . but she was standing right in front of me! Yes . . . Yes . . . Yes . . . Oh, I see . . . Thank you."

She hung up the phone, confused and silent.

"Well?"

"That was the plumber."

"The plumber!"

"Seems the Hartmans' Realtor sent him. The family refused to move into the new home until they had brand-new pipes. They're still living in their house . . . in Utah."

"But I just saw her yesterday!"

"So did I." She frowned.

"Then who was the girl I talked to at school?"

"Who was the girl I talked to at school? Oh, my! You must not tell anyone about this. Oh, dear, oh, dear! This could mean my job!"

Who was this angel girl? Where was this angel girl? And would I ever find out?

I fingered the necklace in my pocket, more confused than ever.

"You've been zoned, man," Chainsaw said at the Seaside Pier Arcade, after I filled him in. "Totally *Twilight Zoned*! Like now I think maybe we all dreamed it."

"It's a nightmare to me," I said. "I see her underwater, then I don't. I see her at school, then I don't. I see her at the pier, and then I don't. Lilly . . . that's all I know."

"You think you know," Robin interjected. "Her name could really be George."

"In which case you could find her on the corner of Fifth and Main." Chainsaw laughed.

"I just want to wake up a couple years from now. Then maybe all this'll somehow make sense."

"You can't sleep. The fireworks are tonight," Chainsaw said cheerfully.

"Are you kidding? I'm not going!"

"Sure you are, dude! It's summer's first blow-out. You have to go."

"I'll be there," Robin reminded me. "I'm the one woman in your life that doesn't disappear."

"I appreciate that." I sighed, giving her a hug.

"I'll pick you up at eight," Chainsaw commanded.

Lilly

I woke up, groggy, lying in the sand. The sound of head-banging music was ringing in my ears. Where was I? Oh, yeah! Now my mission, my love, my legs—everything was coming back to me. I squinted into the pastel sunset and sat up slowly, afraid of looking at my tail. Afraid I may go into shock if it was missing again. Even though it had happened before, it wasn't any less scary now.

At least this time I came prepared in the clothing department. I had strapped on three tops, and two skirts weighed down by a million shells. One top and one skirt safely made it through the transformation.

Something seemed different about the time of day, however. The moon was much higher in the sky. That

damn gold dust! Madame Pearl had said it might make me sleepy.

Earthkids were draped on the pier and clustered on the beach like stars in a midnight sky. Hundreds of kids talking, singing, dancing, running wild. How was I ever supposed to find Spencer in this crowd?

I spotted a girl in dark clothes that I thought I recognized from Seaside High. "Have you seen Spencer?" I asked, tapping her on the shoulder.

"Spencer who?" she answered, turning around. Only it wasn't a girl in dark clothes, after all. It was a guy!

"Have you seen Spencer?" I asked a clean-cut man.

"Is that his name?" the man answered, relieved. "He's been sitting over there with my wife. Totally whining, looking everywhere for you!"

I eagerly followed the man. But sitting next to his girlfriend wasn't my Earthlove. It was a dog!

"Have you seen Spencer? He's not an animal, he goes to Seaside High," I asked a teenaged couple.

"They're all animals at Seaside," the girl answered, as her athletic boyfriend grabbed her. "Get off already," the girl said playfully to her snuggling mate as they walked on. "Seaside has its own section," she called back, pointing to the hill. "Most of the kids from school are up there—the snacks are free!"

I gazed out into the sea of teenagers, and then to

the setting sun. Darkness was not far off. Even in broad daylight, I would have little chance of finding him. The approaching tide inched farther up the shore, tempting me to return.

Spencer

I was pulling my empty Styrofoam cup apart, its former carbonated caramel-colored high-fructose contents forming acid in my already upset stomach. I was hanging on Seaside High's front lawn, sitting on a bench, oblivious to the exciting festival around me.

Brightly colored lanterns hung over Seaside's entrance, between the trees and around the statues, with a spectacular view of the ocean below. Gutsy dancers bopped on the lawn around the flagpole. A makeshift tiki hut housed a snack bar, and speakers hung from the palm trees cranking out top-forty tunes from the master DJ on the pier as we awaited the annual fireworks.

Fireworks. That's how I felt about Lilly, exploding emotion, romantic reds, beloved blues, passionate purples bursting through a darkened world.

But I feared the only thing was exploding was my heart.

Chainsaw approached with Robin, who was decked out in a tight red dress and hipster boots. Radical for her, as she normally hid her body beneath dark cloaks from medieval times.

"Here, eat this!" Chain said, tossing me a bag of chips. "You need some nourishment."

"Yeah. You're not attractive when you're depressed," Robin teased.

"Can you believe the way she looks?" Chainsaw whispered, sitting next to her. "Like we had a total babe underneath our noses all along!"

"Yeah—we did." I sighed.

"It's going to be a stellar—" Chainsaw started. He stared past me, suddenly silent.

"Have the fireworks started?" I asked, not wanting to look.

"They have for you!" he answered. "Dude, turn around!"

"I'm too tired for one of your jokes," I said.

Chain grabbed my jaw and turned my head toward the tiki hut.

It was Lilly—standing only a feet away. In all her

beauty, searching the crowd, in a red sequined halter top and a white flowing skirt with dangling seashells. She was sandy, and barefoot.

"Lilly," I exclaimed, overjoyed and confused. "Lilly!"

She turned toward me, and smiled radiantly when she recognized me.

"Spencer!" she said breathlessly, running toward me.

I held the necklace out to her, but she shook her head and hugged me hard. I wasn't about to let go.

"I missed you," Lilly said, looking up. Her words rained magic on me.

"But where did you—"

"Let's not talk now," she said, placing her salty finger on my lips.

There are some people who touch you and you know they are yours—or if not, they should be. Not as a possession, but as an extension of yourself. Adding, enhancing, liberating the real you with their touch, their aura, their spirit.

She had already left me twice. But for some reason she kept coming back. Whoever she really was, at least she was with me now.

Lilly grabbed my hand and pulled me underneath the stars and stripes. We held each other close while the DJ played "Baby, It's You."

Our embrace was magical, different from any other—not that I had done much slow dancing in my fifteen years. But this dance was different. Although I didn't know much about Lilly, I felt I knew everything. It was as if I could feel her soul press through her body into mine as we held each other tight.

Suddenly a rocket shot into the air, and a explosion of red showered down, reaching over the sea.

"The city of Seaside and KGMS Radio proudly present Seaside's tenth annual Festival of Fireworks," the DJ's voice blared through our radios.

"Come on!" I said, grabbing her hand. Our hands fit so nicely together, as if they were made for the sole purpose of binding us. We raced down to the crowded beachfront and found an empty spot on the rocks jutting out from the pier.

Chainsaw and Robin followed and we all lay back, staring at the confetti-colored night sky.

"Ouch," Lilly said suddenly, pulling at her side.

"Are you okay?" I asked.

"Look at that!" she said, pointing up to a burst of golden sprinkling dust.

I stroked her silky hair. The beauty of the fireworks didn't compare to the beauty beside me.

Suddenly she sat up, clenching her stomach.

"Are you sure you're all right?" I asked, worried.

"It's just something I ate."

"I'll get you a drink," Chainsaw offered, uncharacteristically polite. "Come on, Robin."

"Do you want me to take you home?" I asked.

"I am home." She smiled, resting her head on my shoulder.

"Are you a runaway?" I asked, concerned.

"I'm not running away. I'm running to . . . We're connected, you and I," she said, looking up at me.

"My life hasn't been the same ever since you saved me."

"Neither has mine. The rhythm of the sea is different. I feel a peaceful surf when we're together and a storm inside my heart when we're apart."

Lilly spoke so poetically!

I wanted to tell her how much she meant to me, but I felt she already knew. This was good, because suddenly Chainsaw and Robin returned, invading our love space.

"If this doesn't settle your stomach, we'll try something else," Chainsaw said, plopping down a two-liter of Coke.

I opened it for her. She drank the whole two-liter in one gulp!

"Wow, girl!" Chainsaw exclaimed. "You drink like a fish!"

"Lilly!" a voice shouted. "Lilly! Where are you?"

Suddenly a barefoot girl with a seashell skirt like Lilly's and seashells woven tightly into her black hair was stumbling toward us on the rocks.

"Oh, no!" Lilly exclaimed, as if she were seeing a ghost. "I can't believe it!"

Lilly

Waverly caught sight of me and stumbled over to us. "Lilly, it's time to come home!" she demanded.

She was frustrated and angry. I imagined her going to the spooky Underworld by herself, handing over her savings to Madame Pearl, waking up terrified on the beach, nearly trampled by throngs of Earthees. Finless, friendless, lost without her family or Tide. Crawling and stumbling her way amongst lower life forms in pursuit of a rebellious teenager.

"Look at the sky, Wave!" I exclaimed. "Fireworks!"

"Is this a friend of yours?" Spencer asked, puzzled.

"Wave, you shouldn't have come."

"Let's go!" she demanded, taking my hand.

"I'll go back after the fireworks," I said, gazing up at the electric sky.

Waverly crouched in front of me, blocking my gaze with her own. "Swear on Bubbles' life?"

I stared into her furious eyes, but then turned back to the sky.

"I thought so! You're not coming back—"

"No," I whispered. "I'm not coming back."

I surprised myself with my decision.

"Lilly, what's going on?" Spencer demanded.

"You mean he doesn't know?" Waverly realized, shocked, suddenly rising to her feet.

"Know what?"

"Where her real home is—"

I jumped up and covered Waverly's mouth with my hand, but she pushed me away.

"I'd like to know, too," Chain interrupted.

Suddenly I felt a sharp pain in my side. "I need to go."

"You're going to leave me?" Wave asked, exasperated.

I gazed at the electric colors reaching through the sky like the legs of an octopus. "But I don't want to go."

"Have you thought about your parents? Bubbles? The ocean?" she continued, grabbing my free hand.

"Bubbles?" Chainsaw wondered. "Is she cute?"

"She's a dolphin!" Wave replied.

"Waverly!"

"A dolphin?" Chainsaw asked curiously.

Waverly grabbed my arm and began dragging me toward the water. "Think now, act later! You haven't changed," Wave said, out of breath. "Boy, are these legs awkward."

I looked back at a confused Spencer, who was standing with his friends.

"What do you mean I haven't changed?" I asked, impressed by her sudden energy and passion. I didn't resist her desperate grip but hoped to reason with her.

"Think now, act later," she repeated. "You haven't grown up."

"I feel something I've never felt before, something that was missing in my life."

"You're still a little girl, Waterlilly! Impulsive, irresponsible, immature!"

Her words stung me like a man-of-war. I thought my decision to stay on earth meant that I was growing up. Was it instead a sign that I hadn't?

I felt another sharp pain and doubled over. Purple particles rose over the pier and flickered throughout the sky. I turned around and found Spencer standing behind me. His eyes looked lost. "I have to go," I said reluctantly.

"But you just got here. Here, I'll take you home." He

took me by the hand. "But you have to tell me where that is! You've left me twice. A third time might mean . . . I'm afraid if I let you go, I'll never see you again."

I caressed his hand as my eyes welled with tears. But Waverly's grasp was stronger and she pulled me away, leading me underneath the pier, away from the crowd toward the end of the rocks.

The next moment seemed to last a lifetime, and yet there wasn't even time to say good-bye. I wanted to hold Spencer, to kiss him, to see the fireworks forever reflected in his eyes. I wanted to explain everything, to give him the answers he deserved, to tell him that I loved him. But Waverly's words echoed in my mind. How long had I known him? Even though my heart answered "forever," my head answered "only two days." I'd breathed water all my life but only air for such a short time. It was like a dream. Hadn't I always acted immaturely, selfishly, spontaneously? It was irrational to think I could leave my world for his.

The shooting pain in my side wasn't as sharp as the pain exploding in my heart.

Spencer

uddenly Waverly and Lilly dove into the water as if they were dolphins. I rushed to the edge of the rocks like a crazed animal in search of prey. Why were they swimming? Didn't they know how dangerous it was to swim at night?

"Lilly!" I shouted. "Lilly! Where are you?" I cried against the blasting music but it was futile.

I stared out to sea with a sinking feeling. "Lilly!" I called again. "Lilly!"

Suddenly Waverly's head popped above the surface, and then, a moment later, much to my relief, so did Lilly's.

In an instant she was treading water below me, next to the jutting rock beneath my feet. She swam so quickly! What were they swimming away from, or to? Why were they risking their lives? But none of the questions that raced through my mind in those desperate moments could have prepared me for the answer, when five huge white sonic boom fireworks hit simultaneously, lighting up the sky, the boardwalk, the beach and—Lilly. From head to toe, or should I say fin?

The reality hit me harder than my surfboard had the other day. She was beautiful, yes, even more beautiful in the water, but instead of legs she had the tail of a sparkling green fish. What I thought had been a hallucination the first time I saw her turned out to be fact.

This couldn't be. I was in love with a . . . mermaid?

Suddenly the images flashed—one after another. A beautiful girl appearing from nowhere under the ocean, not out of breath, swimming like a fish, a strange aquamarine Spandex covering her all the way to her nouveau riche flipper gear. A kiss of life, of love. Mysteriously showing up at school. Noticing the two-finned mermaid at Starbucks. Commenting on the Ferris wheel, "I've never been higher than the rocks."

A mermaid? But it had to be a joke. Yet somehow it all made sense, unreal as it seemed.

"Chainsaw!" I yelled. "Come quick!"

"No, don't, Spencer," she begged, grabbing my foot.

"It's forbidden to be seen."

"But this is unreal— You are unreal! Man, I think I'm going crazy!"

I wanted to show Lilly to the world and hide her at the same time. I needed proof that what I was seeing wasn't a dream, and yet I didn't want anyone to harpoon her and stick her in a freak show. My mind was racing. I was disappointed, yet intrigued. Skeptical, yet excited. My brain was in overdrive.

"I can't be seen!" Lilly pleaded.

I saw the horror on her face. "Stay here! Please!" I begged, squatting down to grab her hand.

She could bolt off, and then I'd really lose her forever.

I turned around. "It's nothing!" I shouted to my friends, trying to ward them off. "I overreacted."

I turned around and Lilly was gone. A moment later she appeared yards away from me.

"Damn, she's fast," Chainsaw said, shocked. "Was that a trick?"

"You won't believe me if I told you—trust me!" I said. "She's a—"

"A party girl," Chainsaw said, nudging me. "She must want you to go deep sea diving."

Lilly must have seen us talking, for suddenly she appeared in front of us, at the edge of the rocks. The supersonic fireworks lit up the sky, the world and her glistening tail raised prominently in the air.

"What was that?" Chainsaw shouted, pointing to her tail.

"She's been attacked by a fish!" said Robin.

"No . . ."

"It's a costume!" Chainsaw said, hitting me in the arm.

"No . . ." I confessed.

"A real fish tail? How did she attach it?" he asked incredulously. "And why?"

"It's real!" I said.

"This is twisted! Dude, did you spike my soda?"

We stood at the water's edge. The waves crashed in rhythm to the explosions in the darkened sky.

"Then what is it?" Robin asked.

Suddenly Lilly appeared before us, treading water. "I'm a mermaid!" she declared, with pride, with reluctance, with relief.

Robin and Chain stood in disbelief.

"This is lame! You're spoiling the fireworks 'cause you want to prank me back for something?" Chainsaw argued.

"You said it yourself when I told you how she saved my life. Remember? You said, 'She swims in the ocean better than you, saves your life, and disappears.' Well, she's not a swimming instructor or a lifeguard. You have your answer now—she's a mermaid!

But you'd never understand! So, go away!" I shouted to them as Lilly swam to the rocks.

"Let them stay," she called, resting her arms and head on the edge of a rock.

"I thought you can't be seen!" I said, concerned, kneeling in front of her.

"I'm a mermaid—not a ghost." She winked.

"If she's a mermaid, I'm an alien!" Robin chided.

Lilly pulled herself onto a rock next to us. Her tail wasn't slimy like I would have imagined a mermaid's would be, like a snake or fish, but rather sleek, sexy even, almost glowing. We knelt, entranced, touching her fin, like we were touching the horn on a unicorn.

But Lilly pulled at her side. "I've got to go," she said and quickly dove into the water like a dolphin. In an instant she was back.

"We have to tell someone!" Robin demanded.

"Or make a video! We could make millions!" Chainsaw said, excited.

"We don't tell a soul," I said sternly. "No one must know—swear on your life!"

Lilly stared up at us, her eyes pleading for secrecy.

"No one tells a soul!" I said through gritted teeth.

Chain looked at me with reservation, then at Lilly. "Spencer, you sure do get into predicaments. Okay . . . I swear."

We all gazed at Robin.

"Well . . . who could I tell? You two guys are my only friends, and you already know. I swear, too."

We crouched by Lilly. It was as if Chainsaw, Robin, and I were entranced, mesmerized by her mermaid spell as she lapped her tail gently against the water.

"Have you always been like that?" Chainsaw asked incredulously.

"Have you always been like *that*?" she asked.

We all laughed.

"I've always wanted to be a mermaid," Robin said dreamily. "Ever since I was a little girl."

"I want to be a scuba diver!" Chain said with a wink.

I knew I only had minutes left with her. "I need to talk to Lilly alone. Make sure no one comes around," I said. "The fireworks are almost over. People won't be distracted anymore."

Lilly was magical on earth, but as a mermaid, she was even more magical, even more seductive. Everyone was staring up at some stupid colored lights, when a miracle was floating right before my eyes.

"I was afraid you wouldn't believe me," she said, sliding up on the rock when we were alone.

"Yeah—" I began, holding her wet body in my arms, her lovely tail draped around my jeans.

"I wanted to be with you forever," she confessed.

"Me, too," I said, pulling the necklace from my pocket and fastening it around her neck.

"But—" she said, fingering the locket.

"Lilly!" Waverly's voice called from the distance.

"I don't want you to leave," I said, grasping her wet hand.

"I don't either, but—"

"I'll never see you again?" I asked, my heart breaking.

She nodded.

"We could meet at specific times," I pleaded. "I could surf out to your home."

Lilly stared up at me with watery eyes and shook her head. "It could jeopardize our existence. And yours . . ."

A cop leaning on the boardwalk fence suddenly shined his flashlight down on the rocks. "Hey, you on the rocks! Away from the water!"

Suddenly I was blinded by the light and deafened by the sound of splashing water. Lilly was gone!

I hadn't cried the day my mom left the house. But I should have. I just buried my head underneath a pillow until seventh grade when a freckled Chainsaw picked me, the kid with the sunken head, first to be on his kickball team.

Here I was with the sunken head again, and there he was again, my faithful friend, standing guard against the shoreline.

"Out of all the girls in the world, I fall in love with a mermaid!" I laughed, but it didn't stop the tears from tumbling down my face as I stared out into the empty waves.

I never got to say good-bye to my mother. And now I'd lost the chance to say good-bye to Lilly.

"I didn't get to say good-bye!" I said, taking off my shoes.

"Are you crazy? You'll drown," Chainsaw said.

"Then I'll drown!"

"Spencer—" I heard Chainsaw yell over the music and fireworks as I dove into the cold night water.

Lilly

The water felt like ice as I fell down into the sea. I drifted like a dream, but it was more like a nightmare. Changing, swirling, gasping. My fin was wiggling, but not propelling me toward anything. I paddled my arms, but something was wrong. I was sinking. I couldn't swim. I couldn't breathe. I was drowning!

Spencer

"Help!" I could hear Waverly scream as I came up for air. She waved her arms in the distance. "Lilly's drowning!"

Drowning? How could Lilly drown? She's a mermaid!

But I didn't see Lilly anywhere. Suddenly Waverly disappeared, too. The sea was totally dark, brightened for an instant, when a firework was shot into the air and exploded. I waited, not knowing which way to swim. My heart stopped beating, time stood still. Why weren't they firing off the supercolossal fireworks that lit the sky like a universal spotlight?

"Lilly," I called. "Lilly!"

I treaded endlessly, waiting forever for Lilly, for

Waverly, for any sign of their location. The next burst of fireworks just lit up desolate waves.

And then I saw Lilly's pale hand, only yards away from mine, reach up for the moon, and then slowly sink beneath the surface.

I quickly swam in her direction and reached for anything I could grab.

"Lilly! Lilly! Where are you?" I called, breathless, scared, tormented.

I was lost myself. The waves crashed against me, bobbing me up and down like a discarded pop bottle.

"Lilly!" I called, getting a mouthful of saltwater.

"Here," Waverly finally shouted, behind me. They were floating back toward the pier. I felt as if I were swimming in thick pea soup, trying desperately to get closer as the waves pushed against me. Gasping for air myself, I finally reached Waverly, who was holding Lilly's limp head.

"I thought she was a mermaid."

"She is!" Waverly shouted.

"But she's drowning!"

Lilly's sparkling blue eyes were shut, her glowing skin sallow, her spirit withering away.

"She's drowning of a broken heart! Only you can save her," Waverly cried.

"CPR? Help me take her back to shore."

"No! With the kiss of love!" she said hurriedly.

"That's what Madame Pearl said—the kiss of love."

"Who's Madame Pearl?"

"It's in the kiss—that's what she said! Please! Help her!" she pleaded.

"That's easy," I said, smiling, but almost out of breath. Waverly handed me Lilly's listless body. I leaned in to kiss her, but Waverly put her hand between us. "Wait. There's something you must know."

I impatiently glanced up at Waverly for the answer.

"If you kiss her now, you'll be a merman," Waverly conceded.

"You're joking!"

Waverly shook her head. "It's your decision," she said, with sad eyes.

I looked back to the rocks where a crowd was gathering on the highest point. Chainsaw and Robin had called over a policeman and were pointing at us while several onlookers stood around them. One man was taking off his shoes. Two orange-clad lifeguards were running along the pier. I didn't have another minute.

The booming fireworks' finale crashed overhead, drowning out the music. Reds, purples, greens, oranges, coppers, crimson shot across the sky like passionate electricity.

Lilly opened her eyes for a brief moment.

"Spencer," she whispered breathlessly and closed

her eyes, fainting away. Eyes which had once sparkled ocean blue and stared through me to my soul. Her golden yellow hair that had so energetically flowed in the water that morning, now draped limply over my arm. Her wonderful pink lips were turning blue. A sparkling heart glistening around her lovely neck as it did the day I met her. Thoughts of my swimming angel flashed through my mind and overcame my being. Hearing the wonderful sound of her sweet laughter at the peak of the Ferris wheel, seeing a thousand enchanting Lillys in the Hall of Mirrors. Dancing around under the flagpole, her gentle arms around me. Saying she had come back for me, telling me she was home.

The greatest gift I'd ever been given, I held in my arms. She had saved me, and now it was time for me to save her.

I took a deep breath, and I kissed her lips. Lips once full of life, once full of love. Her eyes opened.

I didn't have to say good-bye, after all. In fact, I was just beginning to say hello.

That night, I saved a mermaid.

And, that night—I saved myself.

I am very grateful to
Katherine Brown Tegen,
my fabulous editor, for her expertise,
friendship, and faith in my work.
And special thanks to Julie Hittman
and the staff at HarperCollins.
—E.S.